# BLACK MAGICK

by

J.E. Taylor

# Black Magick © April 2024 by J.E. Taylor

# BLACK MAGICK

What was supposed to be a relaxing weekend in New York City turns sour when she meets a familiar stranger who freezes the blood in her veins. The experience shocks her world, and sends her into a flurry of doubt over everything in her life, from her current relationship, to her skills as a witch.

Did she truly banish a ghost, or just transplant him into a different body...a body primed for revenge?

*NOTE:* If you have any triggers, or issues with dark situations, group action, coercion, and violence, then *Magick Trilogy* is not for you. But if you like a little kink in your style and aren't afraid of a dark undertone in your stories, then, by all means, pick up the book... if you dare.

# Black Magick
# Chapter 1

WHAT THE HELL are we doing here?" Austin Shelton asked as Paige shut off the ignition in front of a Tarot and Crystal Readings shop in Chinatown.

Paige Turner stepped out of the car and ducked down to meet his questioning gaze. With a snap of her head, her long dark hair shifted out of her face, revealing the crystal blue eyes that always melted through his frustration.

"I need to get a few things. You can wait here if you'd like." She flashed a smile and closed the door on any further conversation.

Austin glanced at his watch and sighed, turning his attention to the front of the cheesy psychic shop. Although he knew her magic practices had saved his ass in the past, right now, he had less than thirty minutes to get across the city to Cornell, and if he was late, he could kiss his chances at getting in to his first choice of medical schools goodbye. He had a backup plan just in case, and that interview wasn't until the end of the day at Columbia.

The fact Paige was dicking around at a psychic's place of business set the burn in his already twitchy stomach on overdrive. Another glance at his watch and he reached for the door. All he had to do was swing the metal open, and she came trotting back out with a smile and a little bag in her hand.

He took a deep breath, trying to calm his nerves, but they were as untamed as a toddler's hair. She slid into the driver's seat and handed the bag to him.

"For luck," she said in that breathless tone that stalled his brain.

Austin blinked and glanced in the bag at the small crystal that connected two strands of silver.

"What am I supposed to do with this?"

She gave him a cursory glance before she pulled out into the thick city traffic, navigating the streets like a veteran cab driver. It both impressed and terrified him.

"It's a necklace. You should wear it to the interview."

He rolled his eyes and glanced out the window. Despite their recent past, he still didn't know if he could put stock in her psychic mojo, but he sighed and fished the necklace out of the bag. It wasn't gaudy, but it wasn't very masculine, either. He slipped it over his head and tucked it under his dress shirt, forcing a thank you from his lips.

Paige navigated the car into a parking spot across the street from the administrative offices of Cornell. Austin glanced at the signs on the side just to make sure the parking spot was legitimate and then gave her a forced smile and a nod before he reached for the car door. Nerves still clenched his muscles.

Paige climbed out of the car and came around to the passenger side. She stepped onto the sidewalk next to him while he closed the car door and took a deep breath.

"You got this," she said, pulling his attention away from the building, and the conviction in her voice almost had him believing her.

Austin tried on a smile and leaned forward, placing a gentle kiss on her cheek. "Thanks. Are you just going to hang in the car?"

Paige hitched her thumb over her shoulder, and he glanced up at the Starbucks sign across the street.

"I'll be over there nursing a Cafe Mocha and finishing up my paper." Paige gave her laptop bag a pat. "Just relax and be yourself," she added, and gave his hand a squeeze before she turned, heading towards her destination.

Austin waited until she was safely inside the coffee shop before he stepped toward the admissions building. Taking a deep breath, he crossed the street and opened the door to what he hoped was the start of a bright future.

# Black Magick
# Chapter 2

PAIGE GRABBED A coffee, set herself up at the table next to the window, and sat facing the door. She spread her notes out and set up her laptop, getting comfortable for the hour or so she expected Austin to be in his interview.

Every time the bell above the door jingled, her gaze was drawn to the people entering the coffee shop, and then she would get back to her paper. Considering Starbucks was across from the medical school campus, the bell jangled more often than not. Even though the waiting line wrapped around the small shop, the seating was sparsely populated, so Paige didn't feel like she was imposing.

Her fingers flew on the keyboard, and her gaze dropped to the clock in the bottom corner of the screen. It had been over an hour and her paper was almost finished. Her gaze bounced to the door as the bell dinged again, and her hands froze over the keys.

His bright green eyes locked on hers, and he stopped before he got to the counter. The familiar stare penetrated her, and Paige swallowed hard. The moment passed when the new patron moved his gaze away from hers and stepped to the counter.

Paige couldn't pull her eyes away from the stranger. His dark hair fell in soft waves past his shoulders, and his profile was equivalent to a Greek god with a perfectly clear olive complexion and chiseled cheekbones that most girls would swoon over. But it was the eyes that had Paige's gaze glued to the man.

The only time she'd seen eyes that green was when Hunter Garrett had possessed Austin. Her chest tightened when the stranger took the far table at the window and sat facing her. His eyes flashed in her direction, and she dropped her gaze to her computer. Heat filled her cheeks at being caught staring, but a quick glance found him hidden behind an open *Wall Street Journal.*

After a few moments, the corner folded down, and she was caught again. Her heart slammed in her chest, and she barely remembered to press save on her computer before she closed the laptop. In a flurry, she swept her papers together and shoved everything into her computer bag.

Chancing a glance, she caught a smirk on the stranger's face as he watched her flustered behavior. He folded the paper onto the table and leaned back in the chair, studying her with fascination.

She scrambled out of her seat, only to realize the path out the door took her within arm's reach of the stranger. Paige couldn't catch her breath, and a cold fear wrapped around her heart, squeezing at the thoughts rampaging through her head.

Thoughts of banishing Hunter.

What if she had failed?

Her feet moved without permission, and the moment she stepped into reach, his hand wound around her wrist.

"Do I know you?" he asked.

The foreign lilt in his voice should have soothed her, but it just made the fear settle into her bones, creating a dull ache through her entire form.

She shook her head but found she could not tear her eyes from his as they studied her before narrowing just enough for the spit in her mouth to dry. He still gripped her wrist, and the physical contact unsettled her even more than his cautious study of her.

"Are you sure?"

She forced a smile and pulled her wrist out of his grip. "I'm sure," she said and didn't wait for him to speak again. Instead, she bolted out the door with her bag and slammed right into Austin, nearly knocking them both over on the sidewalk.

Austin caught her, steadying her on her feet before she looked up at him.

"You look like you've seen a ghost," he said.

She pulled him towards the car without acknowledging his comment. For both of them, his words were not just the usual cliché. And he pulled her to a stop at the curb behind their car.

"What is wrong?" he asked.

Paige met his gaze, uttering a high-pitched squeak of a laugh.

"Excuse me," a voice from behind them said, and Paige froze. "But you left your pocketbook on the chair where you were sitting."

Austin's brow creased and Paige turned, meeting the stranger's gaze.

"I thought you might need it." He extended the purse to her.

"Thank you," she said and took the offering.

"Are you sure we haven't met before?" he asked, and his head cocked to the side like a curious German Shepherd.

"I'm sure."

Austin put his hands on Paige's shoulders and the stranger raised his gaze from Paige to him. The tightening of Austin's grip told her enough, and she gave the stranger a smile.

"We really have to go," she said and headed to the parking lot. Neither she nor Austin said anything until she was in the city's thick traffic, heading toward the hotel that they'd booked near Columbia.

"Was that... Hunter?" Austin asked, his hands clenched into tight fists.

Paige glanced at his stony profile. He didn't look her way.

"I don't know," she said. "He just asked if we had met before."

Austin huffed and glanced out the passenger window, crossing his arms. "Is that why you were running out of there like the place was on fire?"

Paige pulled into the hotel valet service and put the car in park before she glanced at Austin. "He scared the hell out of me."

Austin swung a deadly glare in her direction. "I thought you banished him."

"I did." Despite her words, doubt colored her voice.

A knock on her window interrupted them and she turned, staring into the dark eyes of the hotel valet.

# Black Magick
# Chapter 3

A S SOON AS the hotel door closed behind them and their suitcases were stowed on the luggage racks, Austin took a seat on the end of the bed and stared at her with a sigh.

"If it is him..." His gaze dropped to his hands and Paige stepped closer, tilting his chin up so he would look at her.

"Maybe we freaked out over nothing," she said. "How'd the interview go?"

His lips curved into a smile. "Nice change of subject."

Paige's cheeks flushed with heat. "Well, I'd rather talk about something pleasant instead of Hunter." Just the mention of his name brought a rash of gooseflesh across her arms, and she shivered.

Austin studied her. "The interview went well," he finally said, but he remained stoic. "They said I'd hear before the end of the semester." His hands moved to her waist, pulling her closer. "If it was him..." He licked his lips, keeping his gaze locked with hers. "What does that mean...for us?"

His uneasiness struck Paige as odd, especially since he seemed to have set the pace of their entire relationship. After she was released from the hospital, he had hooked her up with an apartment in the same building he lived in. Despite their sexual escapades while she had been incarcerated, since they left the hospital, he had slowed things down to a crawl.

The past few months had been filled with a flurry of classes, schoolwork, and catching a dinner or a movie whenever their schedules allowed. It was a far cry from the intensity they encountered while Hunter terrorized them.

Austin's sense of humor was truly warped, and it caught her off guard enough to draw a snorting laugh from her. And the man knew his way around a kitchen. Her favorite dates were the ones where he cooked for her, and then they collapsed on his couch for either a movie or a mean game of cards. It was all perfectly civilized.

His quiet confidence was something she found she relied on, so seeing him nervous like he was on the ride into the city today really blew her mind. And the hesitation in his gaze right now shot to her core. Austin didn't show his vulnerable side often, but when he did, it pulled at her heartstrings in a way no other man ever had.

Paige cupped his cheeks and leaned forward, meeting his lips with a tentative kiss. When she pulled away, that hungry spark she remembered from the hospital ignited in his eyes. His arms encircled her, and he delivered the kiss that burned through her like wildfire. He spun her onto the bed next to him without breaking the kiss, and his hand slipped between her legs, rubbing her through her jeans.

He broke the kiss, and his hand stilled, but he didn't move away. Instead, he met her gaze and whispered, "Do you want me, Paige?"

"Yes," she whispered and went to pull him back to her lips.

"Is it just because you saw him today?"

Paige blinked and her mouth fell open in shock. "Austin..."

"I'm serious. You never attempted anything with me over the last few months, and now you're like a she-devil in heat."

"You never even tried to kiss me..." she started and popped her mouth closed. The anger bubbled up inside her, overriding the burn between them. She pushed him away and sat up. "It was like you didn't want me, either. What the hell did you expect?"

Austin rolled onto his back and ran his hands through his hair. "What is it you really want from me?"

"I want the fire back." The words just tumbled out of her mouth before she could stop them.

His eyebrows arched and he laughed. "You want me to fuck you instead of dating you?"

"I want both," she muttered and moved to get off the bed, but his hand on her arm stopped her.

"Why me?"

She turned and met his gaze. "I don't know. You're funny and easy to talk to," she started, and he rolled his eyes. "And when you kiss me like that, you consume me." Surprise registered, and he blinked at her, but before he could speak, she continued. "I could ask you the same thing, you know. Was your attraction to me all driven by Hunter?"

His lips thinned, and he glared at her. "If you think that, you are out of your goddamned mind."

"Then what the hell is our problem?"

They stared at each other, and then Austin broke out in a sarcastic laugh.

"I have no idea," he said after the laughter faded. He stared at her, his expression turning serious as he pulled her back down onto the bed. "All I know is you're the only girl who has ever made me lose my fucking mind."

His kiss crushed her lips, filled with the unleashed passion that had lain dormant for the last few months. Her mind stalled with the intensity of it and the welcomed caress of his hands on her body that shot her into the land of bliss.

It wasn't until the sound of ripping fabric interrupted them that he pulled away from the kiss. Paige pressed her lips together in a smirk.

"Oops," she said as they both stared at the rip in his finely tailored shirt.

"Oops?" His eyebrows rose as his voice challenged her choice of words, but the smile toying with his lips belied his true feelings about the matter. He grabbed two handfuls of her shirt and yanked in opposite directions, grinning when the thin cotton shredded in his grip.

Paige giggled at the raw magnetism pulsing from him, and his salacious grin was just as infectious as the spark he produced in her soul. But it was his stalk up her body with his hands and his mouth that set her on fire. His tongue swiped at her skin between nips, and the low growl of satisfaction in his throat as he nibbled on her ear took her breath away.

The rest of their clothing came off in a flurry, and he worked the magic she had almost forgotten existed. Austin kissed her gently and then trailed butterfly kisses down her neck and chest and her abdomen. His slow progression down her body contrasted with the frantic and animalistic stalk to his lips, and the juxtaposition of it pulled a moan from her even before he settled between her legs.

What Austin did with his tongue, mouth and fingers set her into overdrive. Every memory she had of him between her legs paled compared to this moment. He took his time, making it a slow burn, and every time she was close to an orgasm, he dialed back.

"Please, don't stop," Paige whined when he pulled away again. "Please, I'm so close. So goddamned close."

He smiled at her, and this time, when his tongue flick brought her to the plateau, he didn't stop. The orgasm gripped every muscle in her body. Her fingers dug into his scalp as her wailing gasp filled the room, and a river of wetness flooded from her pussy.

"Fuck me, Austin, please, please..." She squirmed under him as he continued to play with her with his mouth.

His fingers slid inside her slowly, even as her hips gyrated to make him move faster. He pulled his fingers out of her pussy and traced her anus, coating her with her own juices before plunging his finger inside her ass.

"Oh, God," she gasped.

Austin met her gaze and slowly finger fucked her ass. He was gentle enough, so the movement tingled her pleasure centers, and her next orgasm arched her back with the power of it.

When he moved his fingers out of her, she moaned. But by the time she caught her breath, his hard cock slid inside her dripping pussy, filling her with his girth.

"Is that what you want?" he asked, his voice low and sultry in a way she hadn't ever heard. The smile of satisfaction on his lips along with that voice brought her to the brink again.

Paige pulled him to her mouth. She didn't care that his lips were hot with her juices; she just wanted him to kiss her into oblivion.

His heart thundered against her chest, and a low growling groan came from his throat. His hips plunged once more, burying his cock deep inside her, and he pulled away from the kiss.

"Oh, fuck," he groaned, and his eyes clamped shut. Every muscle in his neck tightened with the force of his orgasm, and then the after tremors went through him as he collapsed on top of her.

The air rushed out of Paige's lungs at the weight of him.

"Austin," she barely breathed, and he shifted enough so she could draw in air. It took him a few ragged breaths before he lifted his head from the crook of her neck.

"Holy shit," he said and sent a soft smile in her direction.

"No kidding."

Austin uncoupled and rolled onto his back next to her. Paige debated on whether to roll into the crook of his arm or not. She turned her head, taking in his handsome profile as he studied the ceiling. Eventually, he met her gaze.

"Can I ask you something?" he asked and chewed on his bottom lip in that familiar way he did when he was not in his comfort zone.

Paige nodded and waited for him to speak.

"If I get in…"

"You'll get in," she said, certain of his ability, and he gave her the look that said he wasn't finished. "Sorry," she added at the admonishment in his gaze.

"If I get in to either Cornell or Columbia, will you move here with me next fall?"

Paige stared at him and blinked. "Did you just ask me to move in with you?"

The way his cheeks bloomed red along with the appearance of his dimples was confirmation enough, so when he just shrugged a shoulder, she couldn't help her own smirk.

"You really want to live with me?" she asked, softer than her original question.

"I really don't want to be here without you," he said and turned onto his side, propping his head up on his hand.

"Why?"

He met her gaze and held it, chewing his lip again. The way he formulated serious questions was one of his most endearing qualities. And Paige felt her lips curving into a smile, despite the heaviness in the air between them.

"You haven't really answered my question." He kept her gaze, and Paige's smile faltered.

She rolled, so she faced him, adopting the same position he maintained, and she took his free hand in hers, giving it a squeeze. "I'm not saying no," she started, and his features hardened. She actually felt the emotional wall going up between them.

"But you're not saying yes, either," he muttered, and went to pull his hand out of hers.

Paige tightened her grip, unwilling to let him just end the conversation this way.

"Austin, come on, it's a big decision, and I need to make sure I can finish my degree before I up and run off to New York City with you."

"Do you even give a shit about me?"

She tilted her head and sighed. "You know I do. But you also know I have struggled to finish my degree ever since Halloween. I lost three weeks of school and nearly failed all my classes last semester."

"But you passed. And you're a month and a half away from graduating."

"I applied for graduation, but I haven't heard anything yet. My advisor is looking over my transcripts and will let me know whether I qualify. If not, I may have to take a course or two in the fall."

His eyebrows arched. "Seriously?"

"That's what he said, but he would let me know. If they're available in the summer, I can take them then, but if not..." She sighed and shrugged. "If it wasn't so up in the air, the answer would be easy."

It took him a couple of blinks before her words sank in, and then his rigid features softened. "So, if this wasn't hanging over you, you'd say yes?"

Paige nodded and offered a smile. His gaze moved from hers to the spot over her shoulder and back before he leaned in for a gentle kiss.

"I need to clean up and get ready for my next interview."

"Did you bring a second shirt?" she asked, and his smile disappeared.

He rolled off the bed and picked up the shirt he had been wearing before they started their sexcapades, inspecting the shredded fabric to the right of where most of the buttons remained.

"Shit," he muttered. "My suit jacket won't cover this." He glanced over his shoulder at Paige.

"What other shirts did you bring?"

"Just a sweater."

"The gray one that I love?" she asked. She prayed that was the one because he could get away with that and just the slacks he had on and still look somewhat professional.

"Yeah," he said, refocusing on the tattered shirt in his hand.

"Wear the sweater without the blazer."

He glanced at her. The question written on his face made her raise her eyebrows in a challenge.

"Trust me."

"Well, I'm going to have to, because there's no way I can make it to a store and get to the interview on time." He stood and gathered his clothing before heading to the bathroom.

Paige picked up her scattered clothing and headed into the bathroom as well. Austin was already in the shower, and she pulled the curtain aside. He stopped lathering his hair and met her gaze, moving to give her access to the warm spray.

The only shower they had ever taken together was the one he gave her at the sanitarium, and that crossed her mind as she watched him tilt his head back to rinse the shampoo away. She couldn't help herself. She reached out and ran her fingers down his chest.

A grin formed, revealing the deep dimples she had fallen for more than once, and he ran his hands through his hair one last time before bringing his focus to her. His eyes shimmered with mischief as he stepped closer.

"I can't be late," he said and maneuvered her fully under the spray before he stepped out of the shower.

Paige stood under the water staring at the spot he had just left, expecting him to return, but the sound of the water running in the sink told her that wasn't happening. She didn't know whether to be irritated or impressed by his self-restraint but decided against getting aggravated. She quickly rinsed her body, leaving her hair as dry as she could, and turned off the water.

She took the remaining towel and wrapped it around herself before she pulled the curtain back. Austin glanced from his reflection to her, his eyes drifting over her form while a smile captured his lips. He refocused on his image, combing his hair into place.

"Are you going over to the Museum of Natural History while I'm at the interview?" he asked.

"I'm not sure. It depends if I finish my paper or not," Paige said, and he turned towards her.

"If you do, I'll meet you there, and we can find a nice place for dinner."

"And if I don't?" she asked, stepping closer. She looked up into his gray-blue eyes and grinned.

"Then maybe room service would be better."

He used that tone that made her knees weak, and she stood on her tiptoes, gently kissing him. His freshly brushed breath welcomed her tongue, and his arms wrapped around her, pulling her against his half-clothed form. He smelled delicious, and she deepened the kiss.

Austin's low groan, coupled with him pushing her away, pulled a smile to her lips. She loved the power she held over him and hated to admit it, but he could wield the same type of power over her when he chose.

"You are going to have to hold on to that thought," he said and turned back to the mirror, finishing his minimal preening before pulling on the gray sweater. He stepped back, studying his reflection before he glanced at her. "I hope this passes whatever image the dean of medicine has."

"You look great."

"Thanks." He stepped into the hotel room and gathered his wallet and his leather portfolio case.

"Good luck," Paige said from the bathroom door.

Austin caught a kiss from her before heading out of the hotel room.

# Black Magick
# Chapter 4

PAIGE SAVED HER work and leaned back in the chair, covering a yawn with her hands. She was almost done and really in need of a change of scenery. The morning encounter with the stranger had rattled her, and then the conversation with Austin about moving in with him had thrown her completely.

She thought she knew what she wanted. She thought Austin was just in it for the friendship, especially with how things had been since she left the hospital. It wasn't as if he hadn't kissed her in all that time—he had—and it was always sweet. But it wasn't full of the passion that gripped him today. This afternoon, the man who had opened her to new possibilities had come back into her life.

She chewed on the end of her pen as she stared out the window towards the park, gauging her emotional state. She wasn't sure she could settle for the type of lackluster relationship they had shared for the last few months, but if today was more indicative of the fire between them, she could see being with Austin for the long term.

She stood and dropped her pen next to the computer, deciding it was time to get out of the hotel room before she started over-analyzing their entire relationship. She sent a quick text to Austin and then tucked her phone in the inside pocket of her coat. Paige grabbed her pocketbook and the spare room key before she headed to the Museum of Natural History.

Instead of starting on the first floor and working her way up, she headed directly to the fourth floor and the dinosaur exhibits. She wandered through, reading the plaques and studying the exhibits. After making her way around the fourth floor, she descended the stairs to the third floor, turning to the reptile and amphibian section.

Most of the female patrons seemed to shy away from the snakes and other reptiles, and Paige had to suppress a smile. The special exhibition gallery on the third floor was closed, and she turned to find her way back to the mammal section.

She drew short as the man they had seen this morning blocked her exit. He offered a knowing smirk and herded her into the closed section before her brain could register anything more than shock.

In the dark room, he slammed her against the wall.

"I was wondering just how long it would take before our paths crossed." His voice caressed her with an icy fear.

"Hunter?" Her voice cracked as she uttered his name.

His light chuckle filled the dark. "Miss me, baby?" he answered, but there was no warmth in the statement.

The way he had her pinned to the wall made her heart thunder in her ears, and all the spit in her mouth dried, replaced by tinny fear. Paige forced a swallow, but her tongue stuck to the roof of her mouth. Her lungs squeezed, making her breath wheeze as she fought to draw air into the tight confines.

"I... I banished you," she said, forcing the words between gasps of breath.

"From your boy-toy and the town, but not from existence," he said, his voice low and menacing in her ear.

A shiver traversed her spine, but before it could reach the base of her neck, he bit her ear, drawing a gasp that fell flat on the air. Her brain registered the pain, as well as the lack of an echo, and then understanding of the cushioning on the wall behind her sank in. The room they stood in absorbed sound, making it impossible for anyone to hear her scream.

"I found this poor soul on the brink of suicide, and I made a deal," he continued after releasing her ear. "I'd end his suffering if he would just let me in. The fool believed me."

His dark laugh penetrated every cell in her body, and the only thing that kept her from losing her bladder was the distraction of the hot liquid dripping down the back of her ear, tickling as it slid along her skin.

When he pulled away far enough, his unearthly green eyes shimmered in the dark like evil cat eyes.

"I've been practicing," he said and stepped away.

Paige couldn't move, but she met his gleeful gaze. "How?" she whispered, for fear her voice would shake.

He tapped his temple. "I seem to have brought a little magic back with me."

Dawning horror swept through her. This magic was as black as it got, and she had no idea how to overcome it. Hunter spread his arms wide, and hers mimicked him. He took a dozen steps backwards and her feet followed, moving her forwards into the center of the dark room.

Paige's mind screamed in rebellion, but her body would hear none of her arguments.

"He likes to watch, doesn't he?" Hunter said when he had finished positioning her. He stood close enough for his hot breath to tickle her skin.

"Please don't do this," she said as smooth rope wrapped around each of her wrists, locking her in place.

"You don't find this form appealing?" Hunter waved to the body he was wearing.

She slowly shook her head. While he had chosen a hot package, it was the evil living within that repelled her. Besides, her mind was on Austin and the vulnerability he had shown her today. She had no idea what he would do if he walked in on Hunter having his way with her.

"Bullshit," he snapped and stepped in closer. His hands found her breasts, squeezing them through her thin t-shirt.

She glared at him, and he pulled his hand away, snapping his finger. A spotlight illuminated a bench behind him, and the cuffs dangling from the seat sent a chill through her.

"He made me watch," Hunter growled. This time, when his hands returned, they tore her t-shirt open, leaving her exposed.

The phone in her back pocket buzzed, and Hunter reached around, yanking it from her pants before typing in her passcode. Paige cursed under her breath. She hadn't changed her passcode for over a year, and Hunter knew it as well as his own. He gave her a sideways glare as he typed a message back to Austin, telling him exactly where to go in the museum.

Curtains drew closed, hiding the single bench from her view, and Hunter unbuttoned her jeans leaving them zipped. When a pocketknife appeared in his hands, she tried to jerk back, but she had no control over her physical form. He used the blade to cut through her bra straps, and then he reached behind her with one hand, unlatching her bra. He tossed it into the far corner and pushed the torn t-shirt back so her breasts were in full view.

"You both will pay for what you did to me," he said, his eyes raking over her and chilling her to the core.

Paige drew a breath to scream, and a ball of fabric was stuffed into her mouth, cutting off the scream even before it began. Then Hunter stepped away, disappearing into the blackness surrounding her.

# Black Magick
# Chapter 5

AUSTIN STOOD ON the platform waiting for the subway, going over the last hour and a half of being grilled by the dean of medicine. The Columbia interview seemed much more intense than the one at Cornell, but he wasn't sure if it was his lack of comfort in his attire or if it was just his exhaustion finally taking hold. He sighed, hoping he'd impressed at least one of them enough to get an acceptance letter.

His phone buzzed, and he glanced at the text response from Paige. She had taken a break from homework and went to the museum after all. The idea of ravaging her in the hotel room was much more appealing than wandering around The Museum of Natural

History. His stomach growled, reminding him that food was the priority, otherwise he wouldn't have the energy for an all-night lovemaking session with Paige.

The subway car squeaked to a stop, pulling him out of his thoughts, and he stepped onto the train. It took another fifteen minutes to reach 81st Street, where he got off, trotted up the steps, and down a block to the entrance of the museum.

He bought a ticket and the moment he was inside; he texted her. The answer came, and he headed toward the third floor, where she said she was. Austin stared at the No Admittance sign on the door and looked down at the text again, confirming this was where she said she was.

He smiled. Maybe she was on the same page as he was since this afternoon's romp in the hotel room. He glanced in both directions before he slid into the room, closing the door as the darkness gathered around him. The click of the lock gave him a start, and when he tried to re-open the door, the knob wouldn't budge.

Austin's internal alarms started just as the slow illumination behind him caught his attention. A single bench lay beneath a soft halo of light.

"Paige?"

"Take a seat," a soft voice purred over the speakers.

It wasn't Paige's voice, and he glanced at the message again, chewing on his bottom lip. She said she had a surprise for him, and curiosity won out. He crossed, trying to see anything beyond in the darkness, but it was impenetrable.

Nerves burned his skin as he lowered himself onto the center of the bench. No sooner had his ass met the metal than cold steel bit into each wrist, locking him in place. Dread pressed on his chest as he tried to pull his wrists free. His phone fell from his grip like it had been yanked out of his hand, and his head snapped up, looking for a sign of who had trapped him in this nightmare.

The light above his head faded to a dull shine, and the ruffle of curtains caught his attention. He stared as a low light illuminated Paige in the center of the stage, bound and half naked. If he hadn't been cuffed to the bench, the idea of screwing around with her while she was in such a compromising position would have turned him on. But the fear in her eyes, along with the rag stuffed into her mouth, dried every ounce of spit in his mouth, replacing it with terror.

A low chuckle filled the amphitheater, and a form stepped out of the shadows behind Paige.

"Hello, Austin."

Recognition set in with the speed of burning fuel. Austin tried to get to his feet, but the handcuffs kept him in place. He let out a roar, yanking at the metal keeping him from protecting Paige.

Hunter's green eyes pierced out of the face of the man they had run into at Starbucks that morning. He grinned over Paige's shoulder.

"Do you know what one of the punishments for witchcraft was in the early days?"

Austin's gaze dropped to Paige's feet as panic gripped every fiber. He only knew of the Salem witch trials when they burned the guilty, but Paige wasn't standing on a bed of wood. A measure of relief flooded his muscles. He shook his head in answer, afraid of what his voice would sound like.

Hunter stepped to the side and yanked a sheet away from a nearby table. The blood froze in Austin's veins. His table of toys in the shower paled in comparison. His toys were for pleasure, but what Hunter had laid out was meant for pain. Austin's gaze shot to Paige. She stared at the array, and all the color in her face drained.

She shook her head, and the chains holding her in place rattled.

"Please, don't hurt her," Austin said, his voice shaking with both fear and anger.

"Oh, I will not be the one who uses these things on her. These are the toys you are going to use on her when I'm finished." He ran his fingers over the sharp sex toys, walking the length of the table until he reached a cat-o'-nine-tails.

Austin met Paige's gaze, staring at the horror visible in her eyes. He imagined he held the same.

"You're out of your fucking mind."

Hunter picked up the whip and stepped behind Paige. "They used to flog the guilty," he said.

Austin attempted to get to his feet, his eyes wide with the adrenaline that pumped in his veins. The whistle of leather through the air ended with Paige's muffled scream.

"Stop!" he yelled before Hunter could strike again.

Hunter paused and stared at him from the edge of the darkness. "Do you want to take her place?"

"Yes," Austin said without hesitation, and the cuffs unlatched.

"Strip off your shirt and then sit down again."

Austin pulled his sweater off, leaving only his light cotton undershirt. When he peeled that off, Paige's brow creased, like something was missing. For a moment, he almost laughed at her concern. She was looking for the necklace she had made him wear that morning, but it was safely tucked in his pocket. Besides, it certainly wasn't bringing him all that good luck she had muttered about.

He lowered himself to the bench, and his arms moved of their own accord, right into the waiting cuffs. A low growl of anger passed through his lips at his inability to control his limbs, and his gaze traveled to the table before movement pulled it back center stage.

If he didn't figure out a way to beat the mental hold Hunter had on him, the bastard was going to make him kill Paige. Truth hit and he locked his gaze on Paige's as Hunter stepped behind him.

"Fifty lashes," he said.

Austin had a moment to wonder if he'd live through this ordeal before the first of the strikes hit, bringing with it burning pain that pulled an unwanted yelp from his lips. Paige screamed behind the rag and pulled at the bindings holding her in place, but Austin clamped his teeth together, staring at her through blurred vision. After that first yelp, he refused to voice anything more than a groan of pain.

The silence seemed to infuriate Hunter more, so each subsequent hit came with more force. By the time he stopped, Austin's back felt like someone had doused him in gasoline and set him on fire. Warm liquid trailed down his spine, and he didn't know if it was sweat or blood. He pondered how the hell he was able to remain conscious.

Hunter stepped in front of him with the whip dangling at his side, and Austin got a good look at the leather straps. Bile bubbled into the back of his throat at the bits of skin hanging from the straps and the healthy coating of blood.

"Bastard," he whispered and raised his gaze to Hunter's.

Hunter chuckled and dropped the weapon on the floor, and then stepped back onstage and circled behind Paige. Austin met her tear-stained gaze.

"He must really love you," Hunter snarled. He snaked his hands around her, one cupping her breast and the other sliding into the front of her unzipped pants.

Paige cried out behind the rags in her mouth, but she didn't fight him.

Rage filled every fiber of Austin's body, dulling the pain in his back. "Don't you dare touch her," he yelled, but it was an empty threat and they both knew it.

"Oh, I'm going to do more than touch her," Hunter said. "And you're going to sit there and watch, just like you made me watch, and then I'll let you fuck her with your choice of toys."

"You're insane," Austin snarled.

"Maybe so, but you'll get off on it. Just like you're going to get off watching me fuck her."

Austin glared at him, and then his gaze dropped to the movement his hand made in her pants. The fact her hips were moving in the same gentle rhythm made him want to scream. He shifted, pulling at the cuffs, but ended up wincing in pain instead. Fury filled him and he bellowed his anger.

"You motherfucker!"

"Let's give him a show, baby," Hunter said, and slowly drew her pants down to her ankles.

When she stepped out of the fabric, Austin's heart dropped into his stomach. His gaze jumped to hers and the pain reflected there didn't make sense with her movements.

Hunter lifted her leg and secured it in a strap that dangled from her bound wrist. When he did the same with her other leg, Austin snarled. He had positioned her exactly the way Austin had in the shower when he videotaped her. And her pussy was in his direct line of sight.

Hunter pulled the gag out of her mouth. "I want him to hear you moan like the slut we both know you are."

"I hate you," she whispered, but it lacked the conviction Austin expected.

Hunter laughed, and his fingers worked her clit. "You love this, don't you," he whispered in her ear and sent a knowing smile in Austin's direction.

"Yes," she gasped, and her mouth fell open in that familiar habit she had whenever she was horny and enjoying herself.

Austin's chest squeezed with the betrayal, and he searched her eyes for an explanation. The horror that lay in her expression belied the quickening of her breath and the hardening of her nipples.

"This little slut likes to be the center of attention." Hunter worked her nipples as effectively as her clit. "She'll cum like a fucking geyser for me. Does she do that for you?"

"Fuck you," Austin glared, fighting the urge to be turned on by her body.

Especially when the flush started in her neck. The panic in her eyes didn't temper her reaction to what Hunter was doing, and the low halogens highlighted the building wetness on his fingertips. Austin could even smell her heat. His cock twitched at the spectacle, and he silently cursed his lack of self-control. He shifted, focusing on the pain in his back as opposed to the heat filling his cock.

"See, I told you he likes to watch," Hunter said, punctuating his statement by sliding his finger inside her swollen pussy. When he pulled it out, it shined slick. "She's dripping wet now." He chuckled and continued to manipulate her with his fingers.

Austin stared at the slow finger fuck. He couldn't move his gaze away from the juices dripping from Hunter's hand, as if every plunge brought forth an orgasm, but that was just the beginning. His fingers manipulated her clit until she moaned, and her head fell back. Cum sprayed around Hunter's hand fuck, and he sped his motions until another cry ripped from her.

"He's harder than I am," Hunter said, and Paige's gaze dropped to Austin's lap.

Shamed heat filled his cheeks, and when her gaze met his, he knew she was filled with the same mortification he felt. The only thing he could do was lift a single shoulder and wince in response.

"Think I should let him jerk off?"

Paige sent a glare over her shoulder, and for the first time since the curtain opened, Austin truly understood. Paige wasn't in control of her actions beyond the movement of her head, and that glare she sent was so full of hatred that Austin broke out into a cooling set of gooseflesh.

"Do you want to suck him dry before he fucks you into oblivion?"

Her gaze jumped to Austin's and then dropped to his lap before meeting his gaze again. The slight nod was enough.

"Slut," Hunter snarled in her ear, and he pulled his hands away.

The fact she made that annoyed squeak like she didn't want him to stop rubbed the burn in the pit of his stomach even more. The chains holding her lowered her closer to the floor, and Hunter stepped to the side, turning her towards him. She stopped just as her mouth came even with his tented slacks.

"Show me what you want," he said.

She glared up at him and winced.

Austin's fists clenched when she leaned forward and put her mouth around the tip of his covered cock.

Hunter smiled and unzipped, freeing himself so Paige could suck it without the fabric.

"Are you fucking kidding me?" Austin asked.

She hummed as Hunter deep throated her.

"She knows how to blow like a whore, too," he said, glancing in Austin's direction. He remained still while Paige swallowed the length of him before sliding her lips to his tip.

Austin pulled against the cuffs, letting the sharp pain in his back drown the anguish filling his heart. Logically, he knew she wasn't in control, but that didn't lessen the fury at what he was seeing. What pissed him off even more was the hunger that sat alongside his wrath. All of this tickled his voyeuristic tendencies, and he hated the fact this little scenario turned him on.

"Swallow every last inch, bitch," Hunter growled and pushed forward as his hands gripped the sides of her head. "Fuck, yeah," he whispered. He moved his hips faster, fucking her mouth with bravado until he pushed his entire length into her mouth, gagging her while he groaned.

He held her in place, and Austin watched her swallow through the wet gags. After a few more slow thrusts, he stepped back and zipped his pants before turning towards Austin.

The ropes raised her back to the original height, and she hung her head, avoiding Austin's gaze as her chest heaved.

"I hate you," she gasped and glared up at Hunter. This time, her voice carried the conviction it had lacked before.

"Well, baby, that makes us even." He stepped away and waved his hand towards the table of toys. "Pick your poison," he said to Austin.

Austin stared at the array of horns, all of which tapered to sharp points. From rhino to elephant tusks, the thought of sticking one of those inside Paige left his stomach turning. The unlatching of the cuffs startled him, but what followed shocked him even more. His body moved, ignoring the pain each step brought forth until he stood in front of the gruesome tool set.

"I will not hurt her," he said through clenched teeth, and a pain shot through his head like someone planted an axe in his brain.

A shaking hand reached out, finding the thickest horn, caressing the smooth surface of one that would not only pierce her but would stretch her to the ripping point. One that would make her scream until she bled out. He fought against letting his hand close around the hard trunk.

Austin flexed the muscles in his back and sharp pain rippled through every muscle, giving the strength to disobey the silent commands filling his head. With all his might, he turned away from the table empty-handed. He still didn't have full control over his body, but he had successfully defied Hunter's will. His hands clenched into fists as righteous fury filled his bones, giving him more power to resist the horrific images Hunter projected into his head.

"Whatever he makes you do, I want you to know I love you, Austin," Paige said.

Hunter backhanded her, sending her head rocking to the side.

The sound of the slap echoed in Austin's head, and the red mark on her cheek left by Hunter's hand unlocked Austin from whatever hold Hunter had on him. He launched, breaching the distance in a flash. Anger controlled him, and his fist connected with Hunter's throat before the bastard had a chance to defend himself.

Austin grabbed Hunter's hair and yanked him down, slamming Hunter's face as hard as he could into his knee. The crunch of breaking bones sent a rush of satisfaction through Austin. Hunter went down hard, and Austin turned his attention to Paige, freeing her legs and then her wrists. She collapsed in his arms.

The pain rippled across his back, and he nearly dropped to his knees.

"We have to get out of here before he wakes up," Austin whispered.

Paige regained her footing and found the clothing Hunter had tossed to the side. While she pulled her underwear and pants on, Austin slipped his t-shirt over his head. The scraping of fabric against his raw skin dropped him to a knee, but his shrieking survival instinct pushed him to his feet, grabbing his sweater and cell phone.

"Jesus," Paige's whisper pulled his gaze over his shoulder. She stared at his back and then her gaze moved to his. Horror filled her features, and she took his arm, leading him towards the far side of the dark room.

"You can't go out there like that," Paige said as they reached the far wall, her voice raw and shaking.

Austin reached for the wall, feeling his way in the dark until the egg-crate pattern gave way to smooth metal. "Help me with my sweater," he said and handed it to her. "Just drape it over my shoulders, okay?"

"Okay," she said.

He winced at the weight of the light fabric, but at least it would cover whatever blood was still seeping from his wounds.

Austin ran his hand down the door until it landed on a push bar. He said a little prayer and pushed. The door gave, allowing them to step out onto the opposite side of the floor near the stairwell.

He didn't take another glance over his shoulder. He just dragged her back to the hotel and bolted the door closed before leaning on it to catch his breath. The shakes that had gripped him after crossing half the distance had now taken hold of his entire form like an earthquake had settled in his core. He grabbed the doorframe to get control. It was all he could do to remain standing on his feet.

His stomach clenched, and he nearly dropped to the ground, but the sounds of retching reached through his overwhelmed mind. Paige was leaning over the toilet, vomiting between sobs, and he stumbled to her side, dropping to his knees next to her.

He gently pulled her hair out of the way, letting her purge the vile contents of her stomach into the commode. When she finished and flushed the toilet, he pulled her into his lap and just held tight, unsure of how to react now that the numbness had finally settled in. It took away the raw burn in his stomach and the agony of his flogged back.

He stared into the distance, his eyes not focusing on anything in particular, and Paige curled up in his lap, holding him as tightly as a frightened child. He didn't know how long they sat there like that, and the silence wrapped around them like a comforting blanket.

Anger roiled his stomach as unwanted images played across the space in front of him. Each moment burned into his memory, creating a tornado of emotions. He would never understand how Paige could have loved that fucker. Not with everything he had seen since the first time that bastard had possessed him.

"I'm going to kill him," Austin finally said, disrupting the quiet.

Paige lifted her head from under his chin. "You can't," she said and sniffled.

His jaw tightened, and he nearly dumped her off his lap.

Her hand reached for his cheek, caressing his skin in a touch that thawed the dark chill that overtook him.

"He will kill you if you go after him. He's somehow harnessed black magick."

He leaned into her palm and closed his eyes, dipping his forehead to hers.

"The only place we are safe is back in New Hampshire."

A harsh laugh escaped his chest, and he opened his eyes. "Bullshit. He isn't getting away with what he did. What he almost made me do..." He trailed off and met her gaze.

Her chin trembled. "How did you stop him?"

His eyebrows rose, and he shrugged. "I wasn't going to hurt you."

"I had no control at all. I didn't want him touching me, but I couldn't stop the way he made my body react." Her head dropped to his chest as another sob bubbled up.

"Maybe a part of you wanted it," he said and instantly regretted the words slipping from his lips. Paige yanked herself out of his arms, and she was on her feet and out of the bathroom before he could stop her.

He caught her fumbling with the locks at the door and pressed his hand over hers. She sent a glare in his direction.

"Paige, how come I could resist his commands and you couldn't?" he asked as softly as he could, keeping the accusation from his voice.

"I don't know."

"Are you sure?"

She spun and glared at him. "If you had been wearing the crystal I gave you, none of that would have happened," she snarled in a way that surprised him.

He fell back a step and slipped his hand into his pocket.

"What does this have to do with what happened?" he asked, pulling the crystal out.

Her gaze dropped to the rock swinging from the chain, and her mouth opened a fraction before her hand covered it. When her wide eyes returned to his, a shiver caught him off guard.

All color drained from her cheeks, and she fell against the door, her features falling into that of defeat.

"He shouldn't have been able to control you at all," she whispered behind her hand. "What the hell have I done?"

"Paige," he started, and she dipped her head, looking at the ground instead of him. "This isn't your fault."

"Yes, it is. I didn't do the right spell to banish him, and I can't fight that kind of power." She met his gaze. "And what he did..." She trailed off, going even whiter than before and her arms wrapped around her waist. "I need to feel clean," she muttered and slid by him back into the bathroom.

Austin leaned his forehead against the wall, debating on whether he needed a hospital. The rush of water in the shower pulled his attention away from his own pain. In the bathroom, her clothing was piled on the floor.

All his training in psychology jumped into gear, and he stepped into the room. "Do you want me to help?" he asked just outside the curtain. When she didn't answer, he slid his shoes off and pulled the curtain back, bracing himself for the pain he knew the water would inflict, but her anguish was more important at the moment.

Paige stood with her back to him, and her face buried in her hands. The shake of her shoulders told him enough. He emptied his pockets, dropping his keys, wallet, and phone on the counter along with the crystal before stepping into the shower with his dress pants and t-shirt still on.

She stiffened and shot a glance over her shoulder. Her semi-glare changed as she scanned his clothed form. A crease appeared between her eyes, and she met his gaze.

Without speaking, he picked up the soap and lathered her back, being careful not to rub the shallow welts on her skin. He concentrated on the exquisite burn each drop of water made on his back to keep from getting overwhelmed by the feel of her skin under his hands. The moment he stepped aside to let her rinse, the relief pulled shakes from the core of his soul. Trails of bubbles slid off her back, mingling with thin trails of red before it swirled down the drain.

In some ways, the cleansing of her body reminded him of their first shower at the sanitarium, but this time, her need for feeling clean was psychologically rooted and not a physical need. All he could do was try to patch the damage that bastard did today.

When she turned towards him, he washed her front as gently as he had done her back. She kept her eyes closed, and after he finished, he turned her and lathered her hair, taking his time to hand-comb the suds from root to tip before rinsing it with the same care.

When he was finished, she turned and stepped into his arms. Austin held her, delivering a soft kiss to her forehead.

"We need to get emeralds and black tourmaline," she said after standing in his arms for what seemed like forever.

Begrudgingly, he unwrapped his arms and turned toward the faucet. Her gasp stopped him, and he glanced over his shoulder at her.

"Take off your shirt," she said.

He slowly peeled the fabric off.

More red flowed into the tub and the room spun.

"I think I need to sit down," he said and slowly sank to the floor of the tub.

She turned the water off and threw the shower curtain aside, grabbing a towel before she kneeled down next to him.

"You need a hospital," she said, her voice holding authority.

He met her gaze. "That's the first place he'll look," he answered, knowing she was probably right. But based on what they just lived through, he didn't want to be in a compromising position again, especially in his current condition. "All we need is some antibiotic ointment and bandages."

"Austin, you need stitches in at least a dozen places. I'm calling an ambulance."

He grabbed her wrist when she went to stand. "Do you really think a hospital will deter him? That's what he'll expect, and I sure as shit don't want you anywhere near the kind of sharp equipment they have in a hospital. He wanted you dead today, Paige."

He swallowed the burn of bile and took a deep breath.

"He wanted you dead by my hand."

The reality of how much Hunter hated him was far more than what he carried against Paige. Death was easy compared to the lifetime of guilt he wanted Austin to suffer.

They stared at each other in a stalemate.

"I think I'm going to need help getting to the bed," he said with a sigh, still holding her gaze.

Paige helped him to his feet and stripped off his bloodstained slacks, leaving them in the shower with his shirt. He wrapped a towel around his waist and shuffled to the bed, crawling onto the soft mattress and collapsing on his stomach.

"I'm going to go get something to patch you up," she said as she rummaged through the suitcase. She pulled on clothing before she hand-combed her hair and turned to him.

He sent a tired smile in her direction, clinging to staying awake, to not falling into a state of shock now that the full scope of his wounds was making itself known.

"Paige?" he muttered, and she kneeled by the side of the bed. "You probably should cover me." His teeth had already started the slow chatter as shivers traversed his overly heated skin. The air brushed his wounds like a blowtorch now that his back was exposed.

"Austin, you really need a hospital," she said again, taking his hand in hers.

The last thing he remembered was shaking his head no.

# Black Magick
## Chapter 6

AUSTIN'S EYES ROLLED back, and his head dropped to the mattress. His breathing was shallow and fast, and his hands were cold and clammy, nothing like what they should have been since he just stepped out of a hot shower.

Panic edged in, setting Paige's heart into overdrive. She knew enough about shock from her parents' car accident. She knew if she didn't get him help, he'd die, just like her parents did.

"Austin?" she asked and gently patted his cheeks, praying he would come to. But he didn't react at all. Without stalling any more, she yanked the phone and pressed the button for the front desk.

"Hello. This is Paige Turner in room 508. My boyfriend has been hurt, and I need an ambulance."

"How was he hurt?" the desk clerk asked.

"He's bleeding. Please call nine-one-one. I think he's gone into shock," she said.

"Please stay on the phone."

Paige could hear the clerk speaking with emergency services and then the phone shuffled.

"What is the nature of his injury?"

Paige stared at his back. "He was… flogged."

A beat of silence came over the line. "Excuse me?"

"Some asshole whipped him until his back was a bloody pulp," Paige yelled, losing her composure. "Just get a fucking ambulance here now, before he bleeds out!"

The phone shuffled again; she heard the muffled explanation, and then the desk clerk was back. "The emergency operator said to put a cold compress on the wound until they get here."

"It's his entire back," Paige said, staring at the extent of the damage.

"Soak a towel in cold water and lay it over the wound," the desk clerk said. "The hotel manager is on his way. When the ambulance arrives, I'll bring the technicians up to the room."

"Thank you," Paige said and hung up.

She went into the bathroom and turned on the shower to cold, soaking a towel. She wrung out most of the water and folded it in half, bringing it back into the room before gently laying it across Austin's back.

He started shivering, and Paige grabbed the edges of the comforter and pulled it over his body to keep him warm. Her brain started cataloging things she needed to do, and she shot back into the bathroom. She gathered up their personal items from the sink, dumped them into the small suitcase, and zipped it up with shaking hands.

She dropped Austin's phone, keys, and wallet into her pocketbook and then glanced around the room for her phone. She went back into the bathroom, rummaged through her jean pockets, and came up empty. Neither her phone nor the hotel room key were in her pocket. She shivered.

With her heart pounding in her throat, she went back into the room and double checked the suitcase and her pocketbook. The click of the door opening stiffened her muscles, and she spun towards the sound. Fear burned through her bloodstream and her mouth dried instantly.

An unfamiliar face poked around the door. "Miss Turner?"

Her muscles relaxed. "Yes," she answered and reached for the chair to steady herself.

The hotel manager stepped into the room and crossed to the primary space. He glanced at the lump of covers on the bed. The slow-spreading red stain on the pristine white linens. His gaze snapped to hers.

"He's really hurt," she said, crossing to the side of the bed and taking his hand in hers again. The feel of it settled, the flutter of nerves overcoming her entire form. "I think someone stole the room key," she added as an afterthought. The last thing she wanted was for Hunter to show up and manipulate the staff, or even the medics.

The hotel manager's eyebrows rose, and then he scanned the room, looking for evidence of the crime.

"It didn't happen here," Paige said, and the worry lines in his forehead smoothed. "But I think the person who did this also stole my phone and room key." She glanced at the door. "And I'm terrified he's going to come finish what he started."

The worry lines were back, but before he could respond, the door opened again. This time, a woman opened it, holding the door open for the medical team.

Paige stepped aside and let them get Austin on a gurney while she made sure all their stuff was in the suitcase. When they wheeled him out the door, she followed with their bag and her pocketbook. Every muscle in her body tensed as they stepped out of the hotel, and her scan of the street didn't provide any glimpse of the man in the museum.

She couldn't see him, but she could feel his evil blanketing the area. She took a seat on the bench next to where Austin lay and gave the medic a weak smile. As soon as the vehicle was moving, she closed her eyes, fighting back the sudden burn of tears.

"He's going to make it," the medic said.

Paige opened her eyes, and they landed on his name tag. "Thank you, Sam," she said, reading the embroidered name. "Do you know if the hospital gift shop has anything with black tourmaline?"

He just stared at her like she'd sprung a new head.

The thought of leaving Austin to find what she needed in the city scared her. What if Hunter came looking for her and found Austin unguarded? The thought produced a rash of gooseflesh that rippled up her arms. What if she didn't go and Hunter found her with Austin?

Deep down, Paige knew she didn't have a prayer without the ancient protection of her ancestors. Black tourmaline would cloak them from Hunter's internal eye. Emeralds would turn his evil against him, and anything else she could get her hands on to ward off the evil she would buy, just to keep Austin safe.

# Black Magick
# Chapter 7

THE STEADY BEEP penetrated the darkness, and Austin blinked slowly, letting the shaded light into his reality. The tiled floor came into view, and he stared, groggy and disoriented. Shifting his body sent a river of discomfort over his back, but it was dull and removed from the acute pain he had felt earlier.

"Paige?" His rough whisper overrode the beeping.

When no answer came, the beeping sped up, along with the pounding in his chest. The sudden introduction of panic in his blood wiped the grogginess out of his mind, and the fact he was lying face down on something akin to a massage table entered his thought process.

The shuffle of feet turned his attention to his right, and when white shoes appeared at the edge of his vision, his heart clenched. Hospital. Shit.

"Mr. Anderson, are you awake?"

Confusion clouded his mind, and his gaze darted around, looking for the person the shoes were addressing. Austin picked up his head and turned it towards the voice after doing a quick scan of the machines in front of him.

"Where's my girlfriend?" he asked, his voice tentative, with all the doubts shuffling through his head.

The nurse smiled. "She said she needed to run an errand and hoped to be back before you woke."

His gaze jumped past the nurse, towards the doorway and the hustling hospital staff beyond, before it returned to hers.

"Mr. Anderson, do you know where you are?"

The fact she called him the wrong name registered in his brain, and his brow creased in confusion. A voice in the back of his mind kept his tongue from correcting her.

"You're in the hospital, and you've had close to two hundred stitches in your back. You lost enough blood that you needed a blood transfusion. Now you have an IV line to make sure you are hydrated, and your next dose of pain medicine will be administered in another hour," she explained. "Do you have any questions?"

He attempted to push himself up, but he only succeeded in propping himself up on his elbows before the pain sliced through the fog in his mind. Wincing, he glanced around to get a feel for where he was. It wasn't a private room. Only curtain walls separated him from the next emergency room patient. He gave the nurse a slow shake of his head. While over a dozen questions circled in his mind, he wasn't sure right now was the time to ask any of them.

"When my girlfriend gets back, can you please make sure they let her in?"

"Certainly, Mr. Anderson." She made a note on the file and sent a smile in his direction.

"Um, do you know where my phone is?" he asked before she turned away.

"I'm sorry. I don't. Your girlfriend left your suitcase on the chair." She waved towards the far corner of the makeshift room. "Would you like me to look through it?"

Austin turned his head to the side and stared at their suitcase, wondering where Paige would have packed it. Exhaustion claimed his muscles, and he shook his head, settling back into the bed.

"It's not an emergency," he muttered. The floor blurred and then faded as he slipped back into sleep.

*"Please don't make me do this," he pleaded.*

*"She whipped you to shreds and you want to take pity on her?"*

*"You did this to me," Austin growled through clenched teeth, glaring at the man standing next to him. His hand tightened around the thick horn, and the man's evil chuckle resonated in the darkness.*

*"Are you sure about that?"*

*He stepped to the side and waved his hand, revealing Paige standing behind Austin, whipping him. Every time the lashes hit his back, blood splatters flew into the air. Each biting connection of leather to skin arched his back and clenched his eyes with a grunt of pain. And she smiled an insane grin with each spray of blood.*

*The vision faded and Austin looked at her bound form. An unjust anger filled him, and he stepped forward, positioning the horn, intending to do as much damage as humanly possible.*

Austin gasped. His eyes flew open to the darkened room, and he forced himself to his knees, panting as pain and anguish shuffled through his skin. The heart monitor danced a quick tune, and he forced himself to breathe. Drawing a breath hurt and he let out a gruff groan as cool air caressed his ass. The open johnny hung from his front, and blankets piled on his feet.

The curtain behind him rattled as it opened, and he twisted to take a glance over his shoulder.

"It looks like you are ready for some more medicine," the nurse who had spoken to him earlier said.

"I would rather not," he said and pulled the blanket high enough to hide his bare butt. The nurse met his gaze with a barely concealed smirk.

"You don't have to worry. I've seen a bare ass before."

Austin let a small huff of a laugh escape, and he sighed. "If you have Tylenol, I'll take that, but I really want nothing stronger right now."

She stepped next to him and held his wrist, checking his pulse despite the heart monitor. Then she checked his blood pressure and jotted numbers down on his chart. He remained kneeling on the mattress, unsure of how to get himself into a comfortable position.

"How long have I been out?" he asked and wiped the sleep from his eyes.

She looked at her watch. "A little over two hours."

His gaze bounced to the chair and the suitcase that remained.

"My girlfriend hasn't come back?" Fear gripped him, dulling every other sensation.

"Not that I am aware of," she said, eying him closely. "The police have been waiting to speak with you as well."

He swallowed hard. "Can you check the waiting room for my girlfriend?"

"Sure. Can I send the police in?"

Austin tried to shift and winced.

"Would you like some help?" She stepped closer, but he put his hand up to stop her.

"I can do it," he said through clenched teeth.

He shifted to his side, but his breath had turned into a ragged pant of pain. The back of the bed slowly rose, and he glanced at the nurse with a nod of thanks. The last shift pulled a grunt from his chest, and he slowly eased back against the inclined mattress. The pressure brought the sting of tears to his eyes, and he pressed them closed, counting until his breath came to some semblance of normal.

Sheets shifted and his eyes opened as the nurse pulled the fabric over him, covering him.

"Are you sure I can't give you something stronger than Tylenol?" she asked.

"I would rather not," he whispered.

She gave him a nod and left the room. No sooner had she stepped out of sight than two New York City officers stepped into the room.

"Mr. Anderson," the dark-skinned cop asked as he looked at the tablet in his hand.

"Yes, sir," Austin said, and the lie tasted bitter on his tongue.

"Can you tell us who did this to you?"

Austin's gaze landed on the foot of the bed as he weighed his words. If he told them the ghost of a dead man possessed another and whipped him to shreds, he'd end up in the mental ward. He slowly shook his head.

"It was dark, but you might be able to find some evidence of what happened," he said and looked up. "Third floor special exhibition room of the Museum of Natural History. I was handcuffed to a bench and beaten to shit. If he didn't cover his tracks, the whip should still be there with my blood on it."

They exchanged a glance.

"Are you sure your girlfriend didn't do this to you?"

Austin chuckled under his breath and nodded. "The crazy fuck that did this looked Italian. Dark curly hair, green eyes. He had maybe an inch or two on me in height. Our first encounter with him was at Starbucks across from Cornell this morning, and he freaked my girlfriend out."

The nurse stepped back into the room and crossed to him with two small white cups. One contained the familiar caplets, and the other held water. She handed them to him, and he raised an eyebrow, asking whether she checked the visiting room without the words.

She waited expectantly, and he downed the medicine.

"Well?" he asked as he handed her the cup.

"She hasn't returned, sir," she said.

Cold caressed his cheeks, and his gaze darted to the cops. Fear bloomed in every cell, and he swung his legs over the side of the bed.

"I have to find her," he said and started ripping at the tubes in his arm.

"Mr. Anderson!" The nurse was around the bed and trying to get him back on the mattress before his feet even hit the ground. "If you don't settle down, I'll have to sedate you."

He sent his most chilling glare in her direction. "You don't get it," he growled, fueled by the fire of panic.

"Son, just relax," the officer said, stepping to help the nurse.

"You don't understand, if that freak has her..." His breath locked in his chest, coming in short pulls, like an elephant had sat on his chest. He recognized the panic attack gripping him, but was helpless to stop it.

"You need to rest. Otherwise, you'll rip your stitches out," the nurse said.

He fought against her logic, trying to get to his feet, but the sting of a needle on his backside pulled his head in that direction just in time to see a doctor pulling a needle out of his ass.

"Please," he started, but the medicine worked fast, turning his muscles to jelly. He slumped back into the bedding. A groan escaped as the pain flared. It only lasted a minute and then his eyelids dropped, along with every hint of consciousness.

# Black Magick
# Chapter 8

AUSTIN WOKE TO a dark room. The silence was the first thing that convinced him he was no longer in the emergency room. He cleared his throat and shifted. Pain flared, shutting off logic for a moment before he realized he was strapped to the bed he lay in.

He coughed, trying to get control over the thumping in his chest. "Hello?" he asked the dark.

His voice hung on the dry air. He attempted to move his arms, but the rattle of metal on a bar left him cold.

He inhaled a deep breath. "Hey!" he belted out at the top of his lungs, ignoring the sting the motion created through his back.

The overhead lights popped on, and he squinted against the brightness. As his vision settled, the door opened, and a bearded doctor stepped into the barren room. The recognition of his surroundings dropped his eyes closed.

"Mr. Anderson," the doctor started.

Austin sighed. He opened his eyes and focused on the doctor. "Why am I in restraints?"

"Do you know where you are?"

"The psych ward," Austin said without skipping a beat. "I work in one back in New Hampshire."

The doctor adjusted his glasses. "You didn't take sedation very well," he said.

Austin's eyebrows rose. The last thing he remembered was the needle coming out of his ass, falling back on the bed, and then everything went black. "What did I do?"

"Besides tearing almost every stitch in your back, you punched the doctor and knocked the nurse over before the officer tazed you."

Austin huffed and closed his eyes. "So, how long have I been out?" he asked.

"We have had you heavily sedated for the past seventy-two hours."

Shock popped his eyes open, and his jaw loosened as he stared at the ceiling, trying to comprehend what that meant. He was terrified to ask the question jumping through his brain like a twenty-two shell ricocheting inside his skull.

"Did she ever come back?" he finally whispered.

"She who?" the doctor asked.

"My girlfriend. The one who was with me at the hotel."

The doctor swiped his finger across the tablet in his hands before he finally shook his head. "There is no notation of a visitor for you."

Austin's eyes squeezed shut. Anguish overrode his senses, and he forced his breathing to remain calm despite the internal alarms. He slowly opened his eyes and met the doctor's gaze.

"Any chance I can use a phone?" he asked.

The doctor glanced at the sheet again. "I will see what I can do, but the police would like to talk to you first," he said and closed the chart.

He nodded and moved his gaze to the ceiling. If he counted the hours he spent in the emergency room, the last time he set eyes on Paige was four days ago. Based on the hospital's continued reference to calling him Mr. Anderson, he guessed he had nothing with him that would identify him otherwise, which meant he was on his own and penniless in New York City.

A plain-clothes officer stepped into the room, his badge hanging open from his blazer pocket. "Mr. Anderson, I'm Detective Connelly." he said, taking a seat on the bench against the wall.

Austin gave him a nod, but something deep down told him to keep his mouth shut.

"You spoke with Officer Petrelli a few days ago, and we followed up on your story at the Museum of Natural History." The detective stopped speaking and leveled a stare that brought a rash of gooseflesh across Austin's skin.

"And?"

"Why don't you tell me?" he asked and crossed his arms.

"Did you find the whip?"

The detective chewed on his lower lip for a moment as he studied Austin. When he nodded, Austin couldn't help the exhale of relief.

"We found the whip and the blood on it matches yours, so that part of your story checks out. Can you tell me about the blood on the stage?"

Austin's gaze darted around the room and then back to the detective. Confusion clouded his mind as he studied his memories. Paige never bled. At least not while they were there together. His hand involuntarily jerked, restrained by the soft fabric, but the metal clanked enough for the detective's forehead to crease.

"She wasn't bleeding when we left," he whispered when his gaze landed back on the cop.

"What did you do with the body?"

Austin's chest hurt. He forced a breath and then a second one as his nightmares surfaced. He shook his head, trying to control the need to panic.

"What body?" he asked after gaining control over the wild beast running amok in his stomach.

"The one that you killed."

His eyes widened, and he shook his head. "I didn't kill anyone," he answered.

"Your fingerprints were on the murder weapon."

"What weapon?" His voice rose an octave higher, following the sudden adrenaline rush pushing his heart to beat a new pattern.

The detective grimaced and opened the attaché case at his feet. When he approached, he turned one of the many photographs towards him.

Austin stared at the bloodied rhino horn, and his entire form shook. The nightmare danced in front of his eyes, and he shook his head.

"I touched it, but I refused to use it on her no matter how much that bastard wanted me to," he said, and his vision blurred. Blinking back the tears, he met Detective Connelly's hard stare. "Can I please use your phone?"

"Why?"

"I need to make sure my girlfriend is okay," he said, his voice shaking in time with the tremors wracking his body.

"Why don't you start from the beginning?"

Austin met his gaze and exhaled. "We came into the city because I had interviews at Cornell and Columbia Medical Schools," he started.

"Who did you speak with at the schools?" Detective Connelly asked.

"The dean of medicine," he said. He closed his eyes and leaned his head back. "And while I was at Cornell, Paige waited for me at the Starbucks across the street. Some guy there freaked her out and followed her when she came out to the car."

"And if I reach out to the dean—"

"They won't be able to confirm," Austin interrupted him and opened his eyes. "Paige signed me in here at the hospital, and she probably thought I'd be safer if she put me under an alias. My real name is Austin Shelton."

The cop stared at him.

"She was still alive when I was admitted, but if she hasn't come back from where ever she went..." Austin cursed the burn in his eyes and his now watery vision. "Please, I need to know."

The detective sighed and glanced at the door before he dropped the pictures back on the bench. When he approached the bed, he pulled the phone out of his pocket. "Normally, I don't stick my ass out for anyone, but either you're a genius of an actor or you're telling the truth."

Austin bit his lower lip and nodded. "I appreciate it. But do me a favor, whatever is said, please don't let whoever is on the line know you are in the room, okay?" he asked, and the detective hesitated. "Her life may depend on it," he added softly. *Not to mention mine*, he thought, but didn't voice it.

The hardness in the detective's face softened a fraction, and he gave a small nod.

Austin rattled the number off and met the detective's dark eyes. He punched the numbers in and pressed the speaker, holding the phone close to Austin's mouth. The phone rang for what seemed like forever, and then a tentative male voice answered.

"Hello?"

"Is Paige there?"

The low chuckle filled the line, and Austin met the detective's gaze.

"We were wondering just how long it would take for you to call, especially since she had your phone when I found her.”

“I swear...” Austin growled and pressed his teeth together against the threat, poised to tumble from his mouth.

The low rumble of ancient words came over the line, and Paige screamed in the background. The detective’s eyes glazed over, and the phone dropped onto Austin’s chest. When the gun came out of his jacket, Austin’s blood froze along with his breath.

Paige’s pleas came through the line. Her promises to do anything he asked if he would just spare Austin’s life burned him more than staring down the barrel of the gun.

Another set of words paused the detective’s trigger finger, but by his expression, he now recognized what was happening. All color bled from his face.

“If you hurt her...” Austin huffed as his entire body contracted in anger. The pain that followed nearly ripped a grunt from his throat, but he controlled the sound.

“Please,” Paige whispered in the background. “You don’t need to hurt him. I will do whatever you want. Just leave him alone, please."

"Paige, you don't need to protect me," he said, his voice soft but firm.

"Are you alone?" Hunter asked.

Austin wasn't sure how to answer that. If he said no and Hunter uttered whatever command he had before, he would be dead in less than a minute. If he said yes, he might still be dead in the same timeframe.

"Yes," he lied.

"Should we test that?"

Austin clenched his teeth, and the detective was able to shake his head. Horror filled his eyes at the lack of control he had over his physical form.

"Go for it," Austin said, playing out the bluff. His heart pounded in his chest and fear squeezed his bladder to the point he was sure he would piss the bed, but his voice remained steady.

"No!" Paige screamed in the background.

The phone clattered to the ground, disconnecting the call and cutting whatever hold Hunter had on the detective.

He stepped back, away from Austin, holstering his gun with a shaking hand. "I almost..."

Austin couldn't help but laugh. Paige was alive and so was he, but he knew there was a time limit on both those things, a limit the shaken detective didn't quite understand.

"What the fuck?" Detective Connelly finally gasped and glanced at Austin.

"Paige said it was black magick." He cracked a sarcastic smile. "You know, a year ago, I would have shit my pants laughing at the thought, but after what I've seen this prick do..." He trailed off and shook his head.

Detective Connelly took the phone off Austin's chest and crossed to the bench, taking a seat. Austin stared at him, waiting for him to speak or dismiss the situation completely.

"I'm not equipped to deal with this," he muttered under his breath. He punched some numbers into the phone and held it to his ear. "Special Agent Williams, it's Detective Connelly."

Austin blinked in surprise.

"Sorry, but I wasn't sure who else to call... I've got a weird one here and..." Detective Connelly turned toward the small window, listening to the person on the other end of the line. "I know you're not active anymore, but..." The detective pinched his nose. "My sister said if I ever had a weird case, you should be the first person I call. And this is fucking weird."

Austin moved his gaze to the ceiling, his mind working at figuring out a way to get Paige out of where she was. He had a feeling they were still in New York City. After all, if you want to hide a needle, this was the right haystack for it.

"I can swing by and explain." The detective ended the call and met Austin's gaze. "I'm not equipped to deal with this shit, but the guy I just called might be able to help. Let me see if I can get you out of here."

Austin just nodded, wondering what the hell had just happened. He had never seen a cop do an about face so damned quickly before and especially with someone admitted to the psych ward.

It took a good twenty minutes before the doctor returned to the room, and he quietly unhooked Austin before he spoke.

"You are being released into Detective Connelly's custody, and I can't stress enough the care you must take with your back. The dressings need to be changed twice a day, and I would suggest you keep your back as dry as possible. You can safely take a shower, but until the stitches come out, I suggest you don't lift more than ten pounds."

"Fourteen days for the stitches, right?" Austin asked as he slowly sat up. He hoped like hell he and Paige were back home by then and Hunter was six feet under. He wanted that prick dead more than he wanted to become a doctor.

"That's correct."

A nurse stepped in and placed his suitcase on the bench.

"Would you like some help getting dressed?" she asked.

"No, but thank you," Austin said and slowly got to his feet.

He shuffled across the room and dropped the johnny and hospital issue undergarments on the bench before opening the suitcase. He slid on his only pair of clean underwear, along with the pair of jeans he had packed for their trip home. The undershirt was more of a challenge and putting on his socks and sneakers nearly made him pass out, but he finally had everything set. He stared at the only shirt option he had in the suitcase. He picked up the torn oxford and slipped it on, but he didn't bother buttoning it.

He zipped the suitcase and dropped it to the floor. Pulling the handle out, he rolled it to the door. The handle opened easily, and he stepped out into the hall.

Detective Connolly straightened and gave him a nod. Austin followed him out to the small emergency parking lot where the detective's car sat. The detective took his bag and stowed it in the trunk while Austin slid into the passenger seat. The drive from the hospital to the north side of Central Park took a couple of minutes.

Austin stared at the high-end apartment complex before turning his attention to the detective.

"The FBI pays this well?" he asked.

Detective Connelly let out a little laugh. "Uh, no, not exactly."

The doorman held the door for the two of them before directing them to the elevator. Once in the confines of the lift, the detective pressed the button for the penthouse.

Austin gave the detective a raised eyebrow.

"It was left to him," Detective Connolly said. "He was my sister's partner before she disappeared."

Austin exhaled and looked up at the numbers. "Is that why you're helping me?"

"No, I'm helping you because I had no control over my actions in that room, and I could have killed you. Your girlfriend saved both our lives, and I owe it to her to get her out of whatever you two stepped in."

Austin's face heated, and he dropped his gaze to the ground, feeling humbled by the detective's answer. His hands slid into his pockets.

"I don't know how to stop him," Austin mumbled.

Before Detective Connolly could offer some words of wisdom, the elevator doors slid open, and he stepped out. Austin followed, glancing at the small entry. The detective knocked on the door and waited.

A man with dark hair and eyes that reminded Austin of Paige's opened the door. The thing that threw him was this man couldn't have been much older than he was.

"Hey, Tom, we were looking for your father," Detective Connolly said.

Tom gave him a nod and waved him in, but except for the brief nod in the detective's direction, his gaze remained locked on Austin. The fact he didn't speak unnerved Austin, too.

"Hi, I'm Austin," he said.

Tom gave him a nod before his hands moved in a greeting. It took Austin a moment to realize the man was using sign language. He blinked and picked up the last letter. An M before he glanced up.

Instead of speaking, he signed "Thank you," much to his host's surprise.

"I can hear," he signed. "Just can't talk without a tongue." He offered a small smile and waved Austin farther into the apartment.

Austin stared at his hands and then at his face, wondering if he really understood what the man was saying.

He wasn't at the top of his game, but no tongue?

Tom let out a low chuckle and walked away. Austin followed into the living room and his gaze was drawn to the amazing view of the city beyond the room. Temporarily stunned by the cityscape, he slowed to a stop, mesmerized.

A throat cleared, and his gaze bounced to Detective Connolly and an older gentleman with the same dark hair as Tom, but with gray coloring in his temples. But that wasn't what made Austin's mouth drop open. He recognized the fourth man sitting in the overstuffed chair. Paige had gone all gooey-eyed when he came on the television, and he had to admit the guy had a voice that could charm the pants off just about any woman.

"CJ Ryan," Austin said in only a whisper.

The sparkle in the man's eyes was on the border of impish, and he nodded.

"Holy shit," Austin mumbled and glanced around the room again.

CJ met Tom's gaze. "You got this?" he asked, and Tom nodded. "Good, because I've got a show to do," he added, getting to his feet. He crossed to Austin. "My brother can help," he said directly to Austin.

"How," Austin said, not meaning to be rude, but he couldn't fathom how they could possibly help.

"Trust us, we've dealt with worse," CJ said and disappeared out the front door.

"Mark, we've got this," the older gentleman said to Detective Connolly, and both Austin and the detective looked at him.

"No offense, Steve, but I'd really like to bag this psycho," Detective Connolly said.

"Normally, I'd say join the party, but from what you said on the phone, it doesn't sound like something your sister would want me to let you get involved in."

The detective's jaw tightened, and he sent a glare at the older gentleman.

"Do you mind if I sit?" Austin asked before exhaustion dropped him to the ground. He offered a slight shrug, trying to hide the wince that followed.

"Be our guest," Steve said.

Austin took the closest seat. Lowering onto the soft leather was a challenge, and he had to clench his teeth against the discomforting pull of stitches. He glanced up at Detective Connolly.

"The only way to catch Hunter is by using his magic against him," he said and cringed at how that sounded out loud.

"Magic?" A soft Irish lilt pulled his attention to the hallway and the stunning redhead standing in the entrance.

He gave a slow nod. "Yeah."

"Now, I'm going to insist that you let us take care of this," Steve said to Mark.

Austin's gaze moved around the room at the parties still present and fell back on the redhead. His gaze dropped to the unique amulet gracing her neck. He licked his lips as Steve escorted Detective Connolly to the door.

"Hello, I'm Raven," the redhead said and crossed the room, offering her hand.

Austin took it and gave her firm grip a quick shake.

"I'm Tom's wife," she added, sending a smile in Tom's direction.

Austin couldn't help the smile at how much love was in that single look. "Austin," he said after her gaze came back to his. "I'm still not clear how you can help."

They traded another glance before they settled on the couch across from him.

"What kind of magic?" Raven asked.

"Paige said it was black magick," Austin said, wondering what the hell he was doing actually voicing this shit out loud. He glanced behind him, expecting to see the detective, but the front door was cracked and all he could hear were hushed whispers.

"Steve is walking the detective out," Raven said, pulling his gaze back.

"Are you comfortable?" Tom signed.

"I'm fine."

Tom tapped the back of his shoulder and raised an eyebrow, and Austin's jaw dropped for a second time that evening.

"He can read minds," Raven said softly, drawing his attention back.

The door creaked and closed, and Steve crossed into the room, handing the detective's phone to Austin. He sat down at the computer desk on the far side of the room.

"Can you please call them?" he asked when he looked up from the keyboard.

Austin huffed a laugh, and everyone looked at him expectantly. "I don't think that's wise. There are three of you and only one of me, and I'm not in any position to defend myself right now."

Smiles appeared briefly on all three faces.

"It's okay. I highly doubt his magic will affect us."

Austin stared at the phone, unsure of what to do.

"Call," a voice whispered in his mind, and he glanced up, moving his gaze from Steve to Raven and finally to Tom.

The voice in his head wasn't the former two. Tom raised a brow, challenging him.

"If he hurts her..." He trailed off, his gaze bouncing between them.

"I can trace the call if you can keep him on the line for a full minute."

"And if he takes control of you?"

Raven pulled out her necklace, showing the details to Austin. "This protects us," she said.

He stared at it, and then his gaze bounced to hers. "Black tourmaline?"

"No, bloodstone, but black tourmaline is a good, strong repellant, too."

Her accent was almost hypnotic, as was the looping pattern of the Celtic knot.

"We all have them," she added.

"Why?" It seemed like the logical question to ask, and it gave him a minute to gather his wits.

"Black magick isn't the worst thing that exists in this world," she answered, and his flesh broke out in a rash of bumps. "And we are specialists in this kind of thing." She pointed between her and her husband.

Austin glanced at the phone and then over to Steve, hunkered behind the computer, waiting for him to dial. With a deep breath, he tapped his number in instead of Paige's, praying he wasn't putting her in more danger.

"Austin?" Her soft whisper filled his world.

He closed his eyes. "Are you okay?"

Silence filtered between them, and then her sigh squeezed his heart.

"Please don't look for me."

He leaned forward in the seat, unable to digest her words. "Excuse me?"

"Austin..."

"Fuck that, Paige. I'm coming after him whether or not you agree, and this time, I will end him or die trying." He got to his feet, trying to keep his cool while keeping the conversation going. When she didn't speak, he ran his hand through his hair, painfully aware of the eyes watching him. "Is this really you talking?"

"It's me." Her voice was soft and muffled.

"I know this isn't what you want," he said, scanning the cityscape.

"It doesn't matter what I want. He's..."

"He's what?"

The phone shuffled.

"Get away from me," she said, her voice barely registering with the muffle. The crack of skin on skin resounded, and a bang followed.

A video request appeared, and Austin stared at the button with dread.

He swiped the controls and waited, holding his breath. It took a moment, but then the wobble of the phone being moved took over the screen and Hunter's face appeared.

A succession of ancient words tumbled from his lips, and his eyes glowed green. A sick twist clenched Austin's gut, almost doubling him over, but he grabbed the edge of the couch to catch his breath.

"Son of a bitch," he breathed, glaring at the laughter spewing from the screen.

The patter of feet heading down the hall gave him enough of a diversion to fight the pain ripping his insides apart.

"I'm going to kill you," he said through clenched teeth.

"Save that anger for your lovely whore," he said, and the phone flipped.

Paige kept her head dipped, her hair hiding her face, and she was naked with thick chains around her wrists and ankles.

"Look at him," Hunter demanded, but Paige shook her head. When his hand reached into the picture, yanking her head back, all pain left Austin, replaced by a fury too big for his body to contain. The discoloration of her cheek and swollen eye fueled his anger, but it was the dried blood on her lip that pushed him over the edge.

The snap of fingers next to him, followed by the chains unlatching and tumbling to the ground on the screen, stunned both Paige and him. She stared at him like the camera was broadcasting on her end as well. The spell broke when she launched at Hunter.

Her feral growl shattered all of Austin's reserves, but all he could do was stare in silence and horror as a group of men came from the shadows, intercepting her before she could get her hands on Hunter.

The camera turned away from the scene.

"I will save a piece for you," Hunter said just before Paige screamed.

The call cut and Austin stared at the screen, waiting for the picture to return, for it to show Paige was okay. Only silence responded.

Austin turned his gaze to the closest person, and Tom's hard blue eyes stared out the window, the muscles in his jaw tight, and his fists clenched. He glanced at his wife and pulled his arm out of her grasp.

"You can't make that jump. I haven't felt that kind of evil since..." Raven trailed off and glanced at Steve before returning her gaze to her husband. "Since I was possessed."

Austin's gaze jumped to hers. "You were possessed by a ghost?"

"No. A demon."

# Black Magick
# Chapter 9

EVERY MUSCLE IN her body hurt. He stood over her like a god, taking pity on his subject.

"I don't know where the hell you got that phone or how you got out of those chains, but next time you decide to disobey me, I'll beat you unconscious." He pushed the hair out of her face. "By the time I'm done with you, he will not want what's left," he added, cupping her chin and forcing her to look at him.

"Fuck you," Paige whispered.

"Is that an invitation?"

Just the thought repulsed her, and she turned her head away. His little group had already done enough damage. When he thought she was sporting enough bruises from their punches, he turned them from an angry pack delivering an ass-whooping to a frenzied group of horny gang bangers with just a few ancient words. They pounded her until each man had their turn at whatever orifice they chose.

Hunter watched every decadent act without a hint of compassion, like she was a stranger starring in a twisted porn flick.

"Get away from me," she whispered, but she couldn't stop him, not with her arms splayed wide.

He stepped closer. "What are you going to do about it?"

She went to lift her knee, but the chain anchoring her foot to the floor stopped her. She screamed in frustration. "What the hell happened to you, Hunter?"

A bitter smile found his lips, but it never reached his icy eyes. "You."

"How do you figure?" she snapped, refusing to let him see the damage he had already caused. While every fiber in her body feared Hunter was right, that Austin would no longer want her after what Hunter had done, she would not give him the satisfaction of seeing just how crushed she was inside.

"I loved you, and you threw me away, banished me from your life."

"You murdered innocent people," she said.

His hand grasped her neck, pulling her close.

"They deserved to die," he growled in her face. "And so do you."

"Then kill me yourself, you gutless bastard," she replied with an equal amount of venom.

The flash in his eyes and the pressure on her throat as he squeezed tighter created a web of panicked heat that spread through her like a shot of alcohol. She tried to pull her arms in to defend herself, but that only rattled the chains.

His grip remained tight enough for her breath to wheeze and her head to get light. Hunter's free hand traced her skin, slowly toying with her until he found a sensitive bruise, and then he poked. Her wheeze froze. Pain radiated from the bruised rib and her eyes filled with tears.

"You should not fuck with me right now, because you just might get exactly what you wish for." He stepped away, staring at her like he'd swallowed something bitter. Then he turned, leaving her alone in the barren room, chained, bruised, and naked, just waiting for the next time he decided he needed entertainment.

# Black Magick
# Chapter 10

"DEMONS EXIST?" THE thought of something more evil than Hunter existing in this world dried the spit in Austin's mouth. Nods confirmed it, and he closed his eyes, slowly formulating a swirl of questions. The one that popped to the forefront of his mind was the one that controlled his tongue.

"Why are you helping me? You haven't even asked what happened," Austin said as he stared at the three of them.

Tom tapped his temple. "Mind reader, remember?" he signed. "And I have no tolerance for that kind of animal." Tom nodded towards the phone in Austin's hands.

"I've got a location," Steve said from behind the computer. The printer whirred to life, and he came around with an address to hand to Tom.

Austin intercepted, plucking it out of both their hands.

He stared at the address and folded the paper, tucking it away until he could catch a cab.

"Let's go," Raven said, and both Tom and Steve stopped in their tracks.

"You aren't going," Tom signed.

She huffed a laugh. "Who do you think has a better chance of counteracting the magic?" she asked.

Tom pulled out his medallion and stared her down without words.

"I'm going," she said.

The fire in her eyes almost pulled a smile from Austin, but the reality of the situation kept it at bay.

"You both can't go," Steve said, blocking the exit. "If shit goes down..." His hands landed on his waist, and he stared at the ground.

Austin watched the standoff between the three of them. Tom's hands flew as he articulated his argument in sign language, and Raven crossed her arms and raised her eyebrows in a way that was vaguely familiar. It took a couple of blinks before it hit him. Raven's *'you-are-so-full-of-bullshit'* look was the same as Paige's.

"Wouldn't three of us have a better chance at this than just two of us?" he asked, silencing the building argument.

"They have a daughter, and if something happens to both of them, she will be an orphan," Steve said.

"We can handle this," Raven said, glaring in Steve's direction. "If it were CJ…"

"I would still give him the same advice now that he's a father," Steve answered.

"Bu," Tom said out loud, and even Austin caught the full enunciation of *'bullshit'* behind his inarticulate response.

"Look, you guys can argue all night, but I'm going after my girl," Austin said and started for the door. He had the address and the pendant Raven had slipped him while he was on the phone. He had thought the anger stopped the bone crushing pain, but it was actually the amulet. Now that he had that in his

111

arsenal, he was sure he could wipe the floor with Hunter.

"Wa..." Tom said.

His full command of 'wait' halted Austin in place. It was almost like the power Hunter had over him in the museum. He couldn't move forward.

His gaze shot over his shoulder at the small group. "What the fuck?" he asked, still frozen to the spot.

"Just give me a minute," a voice said in Austin's head, and Tom put up his finger before his hands began again.

"But..." Raven started.

Tom's hand formed a stop sign, and both Raven and Steve remained quiet.

"Stay here," he signed and stepped towards the door.

Whatever held Austin in place released him, and he joined Tom by the elevator.

"You need me to counteract the spell," Raven said from the doorway.

Tom leveled the kind of look that chilled Austin, and Raven's reaction made him take a closer look at the man next to him. She dropped her gaze to the ground with a sigh and then turned, closing the front door in submission. As soon as they were in the elevator, Austin pointed towards the doors.

Tom nodded. "Yes, I can do a hell of a lot more than just read minds." His mouth never moved, but his hands echoed the words resounding in Austin's head. Tom met his gaze. "And I can do more damage than my wife can," he added. The corners of his mouth turned into a smile that left Austin cold.

"Did you use magic to stop me back there?"

The slow shake of his head sent another wave of chills through Austin.

"How..." he started, but couldn't quite figure out the proper articulation of his question.

"I'm not your average man," he signed, and his voice echoed in Austin's head. "The mind reading and projecting thoughts are just parlor tricks compared to the other talents I possess."

"You know, less than a year ago, none of this shit existed," Austin started. "I was clueless, and a part of me wishes I was still clueless."

Tom's smile faded, and he offered a nod. "I've always known ghosts exist, but I really never considered them dangerous. As far as this shit..." He tapped his temple before continuing, "My brother has always been... special, so the existence of a... supercharged human is normal for me."

The elevator opened to the lobby, and they crossed to the front door, stepping out into the brisk spring evening. Tom waved a cab down, and they slid into the back.

"Normal, huh?" Austin said after he rattled off the address. He glanced out at the passing scenery as they headed downtown. "I feel like I just stepped into a bad horror movie." He sighed and focused on a plan of attack.

"We'll have to scope it out before we go in," Tom said in his head.

He turned his attention to Tom and went to speak.

"Think it, don't say it. This is our best chance at a surprise attack." Tom's blue eyes reflected the passing lights.

Austin gave him a nod.

"If I knew where your girlfriend was, I could do a clean sweep of the building, but I don't want to risk turning her into dust by accident."

Austin's eyebrows rose.

"I can annihilate at will."

Austin narrowed his eyes. What this guy just revealed was a little too farfetched, and he wondered if Tom really had it all together or if he was just fucking with him for fun.

Tom broke out in a grin and looked out the window. "I'm not fucking with you. What I possess is what most people think nightmares are made of," he said and slid his gaze to Austin. "And while I wish it was all just a nightmare, it's as real as us sitting in this cab."

"So demons, magic, ghosts, and freak-level psychics exist. Next you'll tell me vampires and werewolves exist, too," Austin thought and stared Tom down. The slow fade of his smile left Austin as uncomfortable as he had ever been. The half-hearted shrug that followed left his core hollow and roiling.

"Are you telling me..." he said aloud and caught himself before he said too much. If he truly had that kind of weapon at his side, he would do well not to piss him off. He sighed and considered his next question carefully.

"What *doesn't* exist?" he finally thought.

Tom stared out the window, and Austin thought maybe he hadn't heard him. But the minute that thought popped into the forefront of his mind, Tom glanced at him and signed, "I heard you."

"And?"

Tom curled his hands like he was losing an internal debate, but he kept eye contact. "I've never met a werewolf," he finally signed.

"So..." Austin started out loud and filled in the gaps in his mind. He shivered and caught his grimace in the reflection of the window. "Why tell me this?" he said with his hands.

Tom stared at his rudimentary sign language. "I have no idea," he signed back. "I usually don't start yapping about all this shit," he continued, offering a shrug. "I guess I'm tired enough to talk. Especially after the last few months." He wiped his face and shook his head as if he were clearing the cobwebs.

The cab slowed to a stop in front of an abandoned warehouse, and Tom peeled cash from his money clip and handed it to the driver before they got out and stood street side. They both stared at the dark building before Austin pulled out the sheet of paper again. The address matched, and he handed the paper to Tom just to make sure. The hardness in the muscles of his companion's jaw made him fold the paper and put it away.

"They're in there, aren't they?" Austin said, and even though his voice was soft, it echoed off the brick and metal structure.

Tom nodded. "I can't tell if Hunter is in there, but I can tell there are a lot of people guarding entry to a room with orders to kill on sight." He closed his eyes and hung his head, putting his hands on his hips as he did so.

Austin read the physical cues. "Are we going to have to... you know... hurt them?"

Tom nodded without opening his eyes. "Ya," he said aloud, his voice holding enough trepidation to keep Austin quiet.

He didn't have to ask how he felt about it. It was clear he didn't want to harm anyone. Austin only wanted to pummel one person, and he really didn't care who else he would have to take down to do it. Tom turned towards him.

"Ever kill anyone?" he asked in sign language and inside his head.

Austin shook his head. "No."

"It's not easy, and it haunts you for a very long time," he said. "Even when it is warranted as self-defense."

Austin dropped his gaze to the pavement and nodded, feeling tiny compared to the man next to him. He had witnessed murder, and the person responsible was inside the building. Until today, killing had never entered his thoughts, but what this man had in mind for Paige just wasn't something he could let loose on this world.

"If you're not willing to do what it takes to get to my girlfriend, why did you come?"

Tom pressed his lips together, sending a glare in his direction. "I came to make sure you didn't get killed trying to rescue her."

"Fine. Let's get this game going," he said and stepped toward the building. Tom's hand landed on his shoulder, stopping him. He pointed to a broken window instead of the door.

"Less attention. They expect you to come through the front door."

"They are expecting me?"

He nodded. "That's what is worrying me. Well, that and the murderous rage inside you."

Austin stopped in front of the window. "Like you wouldn't do the same for your wife," he said, meeting Tom's gaze.

"I have."

His admission sent a shockwave through Austin, and even without an explanation, he believed Tom.

"And you're right, I would do it again if I had to. But I'm equipped to take on multiple attackers, even without the supercharge. I'm a third-degree black belt in jujitsu. Both my brother and I teach that as well as karate, so I'm not without skills. You are. A psychology degree will not get you very far in there. You can't talk your way out of this one."

His brutal honesty got a rise out of Austin, but it wasn't because he was full of shit. It was because he was so right it hurt. He stepped aside and waved Tom toward the broken window, inviting him to go first.

Tom ducked through the hole, and the darkness swallowed him. Austin took a deep breath and followed.

# Black Magick
# Chapter 11

PAIGE'S KNEES SCREAMED almost as much as her shoulders. All she wanted to do was curl up in a ball and sleep for the next ten years. Hunter promised her a long life of misery, but she had the distinct impression that was just a farce. She also knew Austin wouldn't just sit around and leave her at Hunter's mercy, and he was betting on that.

The men who had accosted her had drifted back into the shadows like mindless sentries, but Hunter crossed the room to stand in front of her. He crouched down and lifted her chin, studying her swollen features with a critical eye.

"I hate you," Paige whispered, issuing a deadly glare.

He didn't speak; he just stared until the silence encompassed the room.

Paige wanted to shift under his gaze, but she didn't even have the strength to yank her chin from his grasp.

"I've dreamed of this for months," he said, his voice no louder than a whisper. "But outside of screwing with you at the museum, this has not satisfied my need for revenge. You banished me."

His eyes flashed with enough anger to layer another set of chills over her already freezing form. His fingers dug into her cheeks, and she kept her teeth clenched against the pain and fear ripping her insides to shreds.

"You will scream for mercy before I am done with you."

"Promises, promises," she uttered. She wondered just when she had lost her mind, but it had the desired effect.

Hunter blinked and dropped his hand, sitting back on his haunches.

The door on the far side of the room creaked, and Paige's gaze moved from Hunter to the tall man stepping into the room. Even from this distance, his blue eyes radiated in the darkness like beacons. His gaze locked with hers, and she almost heard the "shhh" as his finger covered his lips.

Unfortunately, Hunter turned toward where her eyes had been drawn. He stood and turned, crossing his arms as the stranger halted after another step into the room. Austin stepped next to the stranger, and Paige's heart sank.

Hunter uttered the same ancient words he had before. But the stranger's brow knit, and his hands moved. Austin focused on the movement and shrugged.

"You brought a deaf mute as backup?"

Austin chuckled and nodded. "I figured it was safer than being at your mercy." His gaze moved beyond Hunter and landed on her. His wince at her condition was visible to both Hunter and her.

Hunter just laughed.

"Kill the deaf mute," Hunter ordered. "And bring that idiot over here," he added.

The men hidden in the shadows moved into view. Every man in the room carried a sharp object from knives to axes.

Austin's jaw dropped open. The first traces of fear filled his eyes as they locked with Paige's.

Two large men hauled him toward Paige but stopped halfway across the floor where he was turned to witness his friend's death.

The stranger assessed the threat surrounding him before he traded a glance with Austin. The complete absence of fear in his eyes shocked Paige, but there was remorse. He sent a nonchalant half-shrug like this outcome had been expected. As the men got closer, the stranger shifted his stance into one that was vaguely familiar.

Hunter's laugh rang out, pulling the stranger's gaze his way. There was something hard reflected in his blue eyes, something that made Paige swallow the hope that flared.

Austin struggled to escape from the grip the men had on him, but it was useless. He was not equipped with the rugged muscles that tensed under the stranger's shirt. Paige couldn't place where she had seen that look before, and she just stared.

The first clod lunged, and the man parried, knocking the blade from the attacker. He threw him into the line that had closed in behind him. In one move, he took out three attackers, but he didn't have time to recover before an axe swung. He jumped out of the way, but the blade left a clean slice in his shirt. He fought valiantly, with only a scratch here and there. Until the entire group attacked as one.

The man fell in the middle of the mêlée, and a couple of the weapons appeared bloody before they plunged in again.

"You bastard," Austin whispered, still struggling while the men holding him turned him in Hunter's direction.

The roar that came from the center of the attack zone snapped all their gazes, and every attacker fell like a blast had gone off in the center of the group. Everyone was out cold, and standing undamaged in the center of them was the stranger. He gave Hunter a tilt of his head, and then his gaze landed on Austin.

He snapped his fingers, and the two men holding Austin fell in an unconscious pile as well.

Hunter remained stunned and blinking as Austin's fist connected with his face, knocking him down. Hunter got his bearings quicker than Paige could have foreseen, and he was on his feet and behind Paige before any of them took a step.

Cold steel pressed on her throat.

"Don't you dare," Austin said.

"I'll do whatever the fuck I please," Hunter growled, but the knife flew out of his hand, clattering on the floor as the stranger approached.

His glare was intimidating and hauntingly familiar.

"What the fuck are you?" Hunter asked with his hand still balled in Paige's hair.

"Your worst fucking nightmare."

Paige heard the words as clear as day in her head, but the words from his mouth were just a jumble of non-articulate sounds. The venom that came with the words, along with the righteous anger in his eyes, tripped her memory, and she recoiled as much as possible in the chains.

His hand pushed out like a stop sign, and Hunter's grip on her disappeared just before the thud. The man's gaze dropped to hers, and he waved his hand like he was knocking a gnat out of the way. The chains holding her in place disintegrated.

Austin caught her before she face-planted on the ground.

"He's mine," Austin growled, and the man turned his hard glare in his direction.

"Not yet," he signed and said at the same time. He walked over to the table of dark toys and scanned the horrifying contents before reaching out and picking up a simple pair of scissors.

When Austin went to set her down, Paige grabbed hold of him, keeping him in place.

"Don't become him," she said, her voice cracking with panic.

His murderous gaze softened. He slowly scanned the bruises traversing her skin, and his expression turned cold like his heart turned to ice. "He has to pay," Austin said in a tone she had never heard from him.

The high-pitched scream pulled their attention to Hunter, and all she could see were his hands gripping air at his sides. The man stepped away, tossing the bloody scissors to the side, along with the fleshy stub of a tongue. He turned and walked away, but Hunter's scream turned into a growl and he launched through the air. A quick sidestep and Hunter landed face down. The man didn't even glance at where Hunter fell. Instead, he approached Austin and Paige, unbuttoning his dress shirt as he crossed the distance.

He stopped in front of them and peeled the silk off his back, handing it to Paige.

"Thank you," Paige whispered as Austin helped her slip into the fabric, covering up her naked and bruised form.

The man turned his head toward Hunter in time to catch a flying blade an inch from his face. The air rippled, and a burst hit Hunter, tossing him like a rag doll into the far wall. Then the man pulled a phone out of his pocket and tapped a few keys before taking a seat next to Paige and Austin.

"If he wakes up before the cops get here, you can knock his ass out," he signed. Blood dripped from the hand that had caught the knife.

Austin gave him a simple nod.

"Who are you?" Paige whispered.

He extended his uninjured hand. "Tom Ryan," he said when she tentatively accepted the handshake. His voice in her head was clear, unlike the words tumbling from his mouth. "Jackass over there won't be able to control anyone ever again. It's kind of hard to cast a spell without a tongue."

Paige stared in confusion and then looked at Austin. "How come you weren't affected by his spell?"

Both men pulled out elaborate medallions from under their shirts.

"His wife knew how to counteract his spells," Austin said.

"Is that... bloodstone?" Paige asked, mesmerized by the ancient stone symbols hanging from simple silver chains. The Celtic knots made her gaze bounce to Tom's.

He nodded.

She blinked a few times at his sheepish smile, and then the familiarity clicked once again.

"You starred in a movie," Paige whispered reverently.

"No." He shook his head, but the wry smile remained. "Can't act without a tongue." He opened his mouth, showing the stub.

"I swear, you look exactly like the actor in..." She trailed off, searching her memory for the title of the horror movie.

He chuckled, glancing toward Hunter before signing. "I get that from time to time," he said and kept his gaze glued on Hunter. A crease appeared between his eyes, and he scanned the unconscious bodies littering the floor.

"This isn't over yet."

# Black Magick
# Chapter 12

AUSTIN STARED AT him, dumbfounded by the signed words echoing in his head.

"What do you mean it's not over?" he asked and glanced at Paige. Her eyes were full of the physical pain racking her form, along with an exhaustion that was as palpable as the anger flooding his veins. Every time he looked at her, at the bruises and dullness of her once vibrant eyes, his fury nearly overrode all senses. Austin pressed his lips together, pulling her closer in a protective reflex, but her wince made him relax his grip.

Opposite needs yanked at him. On one hand, he wanted to rip Hunter to pieces just to satisfy the growing beast in the center of his being. His need to be there, to protect Paige from what was coming next, to be her rock, overrode the murderous rage.

He glanced around the room, searching for the danger reflected in Tom's tense features. Tom tapped out a number and set his phone on speaker before handing it to Austin. Even before the cellphone hit his palm, Raven's Irish brogue came over the line.

"Tell her I need that counteractive spell," he signed as some men he knocked out started stirring. "They are still programmed to kill me. Knocking them out didn't erase the command."

Austin relayed the message as Tom took to his feet. With three distinct piles of unconscious bodies scattered across the room, his gaze jumped from Hunter to the group that tried to kill him. His greatest threats were the weapons still within reach of those men.

"What's he doing?" Raven asked as silence dragged over the line.

"Um, I don't know. He's just standing there assessing things," Austin said. Tom's hands moved again, signing, while Austin translated. "He said when they wake, they'll go on the attack again unless you can counteract it."

"And he can't make the asshole who cast the spell rescind it?"

Austin gave a sharp laugh—Paige did, too—and he cleared his throat, meeting Tom's gaze for a moment. Tom glanced at Hunter and then back at Austin with a quick shake of his head.

"Uh. No."

"He didn't kill him, did he?"

Tom's eyes rolled, and he signed, "Does she have a spell or not?"

"Uh, no, he didn't. I think you might want to get a move on with the spell," he said, his focus pulled to the shuffle to their right.

A couple of the men were climbing to their hands and knees. When their eyes focused on Tom, the kill command clicked in every wrathful feature on their faces.

"Come on, Raven, they're coming for me, and I really don't want to hurt them again," Tom signed, and Austin translated.

Tom shuffled away from them, and Austin sighed with relief. Being in the kill zone wasn't something he relished, and by the looks of these zombie-like men, that's exactly where this was headed. Paige couldn't move quickly in her condition, so Austin said a little prayer.

"Who are these people?" Paige asked, pulling the shirt tighter around her as she pressed herself closer to Austin.

"I'm not sure, but at least they're on our side," he said, meeting her wide eyes before glancing at the oncoming attackers.

"Sweetie, we'll explain as soon as we get you out of this mess," Raven said through the phone line. Then the most lyrical words rang through the room, creating a silver mist that flowed from ceiling to floor, cleansing the space with an ethereal shine.

Austin stared at the shimmer and glanced up at Tom. The tension in his face had relaxed, and he offered a nod.

"That should do the trick," Raven said over the speakerphone.

"Ov oo," Tom said aloud.

"I love you, too. Detective Connelly is on the way. I trust you can keep that maniac in line until the police arrive?"

"Ya," he answered and took the phone, ending the call.

The men standing in the center of the room blinked a few times before they looked down at the weapons in their hands. Metal clanked on the floor, and the horror of their misdeeds passed over their features. Hands slowly rose to cover their mouths, and their gazes transferred to Paige's. Remorse lived in their irises. Their muttered apologies were muffled by their hands.

Paige gave them a nod, accepting it for what it was, but Austin glared at them.

"You have the audacity to stand there and apologize for beating her and god knows what else? Where the fuck was your restraint?" he snarled at them.

"They had no control," Paige said.

Anger overrode logic, and he peeled her off and stood, taking a step towards the two men with his fists so tight they throbbed. Tom's hand clamped down on his shoulder, stopping him from doing anything he would regret.

He glared over his shoulder anyway, and his eyes widened. Without thinking, he threw himself in front of Paige. Pain ripped through his upper right chest as the blade sank into his flesh.

The blade meant to kill Paige.

Before Hunter could launch another knife, the room shook and the floor actually rippled at the power rolling from Tom. All metal in the vicinity between where Tom stood, and the concentrated area around Hunter shattered into dust.

The men in the center of the room turned and ran like they had seen the faces of a thousand ghosts.

Austin's gaze turned to Paige, and he offered her what he hoped was a smile. He couldn't hear a thing above the high-pitched ringing in his ears and both his chest and back felt like an angry bear attacked him.

"I guess this just isn't my week," he whispered.

Her hysterical laugh, along with the far away shouts of officers filling the room, followed him into the black.

# Black Magick
# Chapter 13

HE TRIED TO swallow, but his tongue stuck to the roof of his mouth. His eyelids fluttered against the heavy pull to close, leaving him with the soothing sounds of a steady beeping. The sharp smell of antiseptic made his nose crinkle, and he tried to turn his head. The motion woke the pain, and he inhaled, opening his eyes to the sterile hospital room.

"Paige?" he asked in nothing more than a croak.

A chair to his right scraped on the floor, and an unfamiliar face stepped into view. It took him a moment to place the man. With recognition came the flood of memories.

"Your girlfriend is just down the hall," he said, but his lips didn't move at all.

Austin tried to speak, but his tongue kept scraping across the roof of his mouth like he had inhaled a handful of granite dust. Without having to ask, Tom handed him a cup of water with a straw.

The cool liquid felt like the richest chocolate sauce as it moistened his mouth and throat. He licked his lips and handed the cup back.

"How is she?"

Tom pulled the chair closer. "She's got a few broken ribs, some contusions, and a slew of bruises. She developed a mild case of pneumonia from the way she was bound, but the doctors feel she will fully recover from her physical injuries. There's nothing that is permanent. But her mental state... well, she's a mess," he signed.

Austin was thankful that he also projected the words, because in his drugged state, he was having difficulty following the conversation via sign language.

"Can I see her?"

"You haven't been given the go ahead to get up yet."

Austin stared at him for a moment and then pushed himself into a sitting position. The room spun, and he gripped the edge of the bed, closing his eyes while he counted breaths. When the spinning stopped, he blinked his eyes, focusing on the floor tiles.

"Can you get me a wheelchair?" he asked, still staring at the floor.

Tom passed through the door.

Austin glanced up at the IV and muttered under his breath. It was on the bed frame, not a mobile device.

*I got it covered.* Tom's thought invaded his mind, and a moment later, he appeared with a wheelchair that had a t-bar for the intravenous bag. He helped Austin into the chair and got the bag all set before he wheeled him out of the room.

Just down the hall must be a local expression because it seemed like a network of mazes and even included an elevator ride to a higher floor.

As they approached the door, Austin said, "You've got to be kidding me."

The clearly marked No Admittance sign graced the doors. Austin had seen that sign so many times in the past, but this time it made no sense.

Tom stopped and stepped into view. "She killed Hunter," he signed slowly, opting not to follow up with the audible in his mind.

Austin stared up at Tom, blinking as the words sunk in. "How?"

Tom blew out a stream of air. "When you passed out, she freaked. I don't know where she found the strength, but as the police were escorting him out, she took the knife he had thrown at you and launched it before anyone could stop her."

Austin's head lowered, and he took a deep breath. "I want to see her," he said.

Tom knocked on the door, and it took a moment before an orderly opened it.

Austin looked up as Tom positioned himself behind the chair. "I need to see Paige Turner," he said.

The orderly looked from Austin to Tom and back before swinging the door wide so they could enter. "This way," the orderly said.

Entry to a psych ward was never that easy. Austin glanced over his

140

shoulder at Tom. He actually winked and smirked at Austin before refocusing on the orderly.

"Where do you think you're going?" a nurse stepped into view, blocking their path.

"I need to see Paige," Austin said, staring her down, hoping Tom could work his silent magic again.

Her eyes moved beyond him, and just by the way she was studying the space, he knew Tom was signing. Her eyebrows arched and her gaze traveled back to Austin's. "Mr. Shelton?" she asked.

Austin nodded.

The nurse sighed and glanced over her shoulder before returning her gaze to his. "I rarely bend the rules, but in this case, I think seeing you will help Miss. Turner." She turned toward a bank of rooms beyond her.

Tom pushed the chair, following the nurse.

She unlocked a door, and Tom rolled him into the dimly lit room. Paige stared out the small window, and Austin's gaze landed on the restraints holding her in place. An intravenous line ran from her arm, and the heart monitor kept the steady beat.

"Paige?" he said and reached for her hand. It wasn't until his skin touched hers that her glazed eyes turned in his direction. He glanced at the nurse. "What the fuck did you give her?"

"Clozapine," the nurse answered.

"An antipsychotic?"

"She wouldn't calm down."

Austin glared at her and turned back to Paige. She stared right through him.

"Paige?" he asked again and squeezed her hand. This time her eyes seemed to focus, and she blinked like she was just waking from a nightmare.

"Austin?" she said in the slow drawl of a heavily medicated person.

"Yeah, baby, it's me."

She glanced at the wheelchair and his poorly fitted hospital johnny, her gaze traveling from the IV in his arm to the bag hanging from the bar and then to Tom standing behind him. When she finally found his face again, he smiled.

"I hear you're a hell of a shot with a knife," Austin said.

She huffed a laugh and started coughing. Despite the drugs, pain traveled over her features, and she whimpered and fell back into the pillow. "I hurt."

"I'm sorry it took me so long to find you," Austin said, and when she turned back to him, she became a blur behind the building tears. He hung his head, resting his forehead on her hand as all the fear and pain he felt the last few days purged.

"Call me when you're ready to go back to your room," Tom's voice echoed, and the click of the door left Auston alone with Paige.

"I killed him," she said with no emotion at all.

"Good," Austin whispered and sniffled as he met her gaze.

Tears filled her eyes and slowly tracked down her face. "I couldn't..." She stopped and took a breath. "I thought..." Again, she trailed off, and the bed vibrated with her silent sobs.

Austin untied her wrist and forced himself to his feet before he took a seat on the edge of her bed, holding her hand to his chest. Her gaze dropped and her fingers moved across the medallion that lay against his skin before returning to his.

He placed his hand against her chest, lightly enough so he didn't hurt her, and smiled at the shape of the same insignia below her shirt. Tom had made sure they were both safe. Even if it was against hospital policy, he wasn't taking any chances after what had occurred.

Her hand followed to his, and she pulled the necklace out from under her shirt, studying it before she tucked it away again.

"I don't know when they're going to let me out."

"You won't be in here long, I promise." He leaned over and untied her other wrist, wincing at the movement.

She sat up slowly with a wince of her own and gently circled her arms around his neck.

They held each other in a loose hug for what seemed like forever until the door opened. Both of them slowly dropped their arms and looked at the doorway. The nurse stood in the entry with her hands on her hips and her lips pressed so tight they were non-existent.

"You unbuckled her?" The question was delivered in an angry screech.

Austin stared her down. "Yes. She isn't a threat. Don't treat her like one, and the next time you decide to give out an antipsychotic to someone, make damned sure you have all the medical facts. She's got pneumonia. Didn't you read the chart?"

"She was just doing her job," Paige whispered, wincing as she lay back on the bed.

"No. She wasn't. If she had read your file, she would never have given you that medicine. It could affect your breathing, especially with pneumonia." He shot a glare in the nurse's direction to find her frantically swiping the screen of her electronic chart. When her face paled, she looked up with saucer-like eyes.

"I've worked in a psych ward for the last five years. I was in New York interviewing at Cornell and Columbia for their medical programs," Austin said. "I know my way around sedatives, and I also know what a mistake costs."

The nurse opened her mouth to speak, and he cocked his head, waiting for the pending argument. Instead, the nurse muttered a soft apology and turned, taking her leave.

Austin waited until the door closed before he turned back to Paige. "I doubt they'll be giving you sedatives like this again. What the hell were you thinking?" he asked as his mind started filtering the questions that had piled up in his stupor.

"I thought you were dead."

Her answer shot the irritation from every limb, and the result was a dizzying exhaustion.

"You won't get rid of me that easily," he said with a smile. "I probably should go back to my room so they can give me a little something for the pain."

"Don't go," she whispered, and her gaze bounced around the room before returning to him.

"Why not?" he asked, but the fear in her eyes gave him pause.

She stared at him. "He's here. I can feel the evil seeping into the air."

His smile faded. "He can't touch you. Not with that necklace."

"But he can taunt me and make it so I can't sleep," she said, her eyes begging him to stay.

Tom stepped into the room, sweeping his gaze from one side to the other, and he offered a shake of his head. Austin's conversation about ghosts popped into the forefront of his mind.

"He isn't here now," Austin said and turned his gaze back to Paige.

"How do you know?" she asked.

"He can see ghosts."

The answer seemed simple enough, and she narrowed her gaze in Tom's direction. He tapped his watch and Austin gave him a nod.

"I have to go, but I'll be back in the morning, and then we'll get you out of here, okay?"

"They aren't going to let me go."

"Yes, they are. You weren't in the right mind..."

"Exactly," she said. "I wasn't and now I'm here again."

"We'll figure it out," he said and shifted to his feet, sliding back into the wheelchair. He sent a smile in her direction.

Tom crossed the room, signing.

"He said he already called his lawyer for us," Austin translated.

"Why?" Paige asked.

Tom's hands continued.

"Because he says he should have roasted that fucker when he had the chance," Austin said.

Silence settled between them, and Paige gave him a nod of thanks before her eyelids slowly closed.

"Love you, Austin," she whispered.

"Love you, too, Paige," he said and squeezed her hand.

Tom rolled him out, and before he rolled off the floor, he made Tom stop at the nurse's station.

"I'm downstairs. If something happens with Paige, please come get me."

"I'm sure she will be just fine. We will keep a close eye on her until the medicine wears off."

"Thank you," he said, and they headed back towards his room.

# Black Magick
# Chapter 14

PAIGE STARED AT the ceiling, aware that the crawl on her skin was more from the medication than any precognition. She didn't want to close her eyes. When she closed her eyes, she was no longer safe, and just the thought of it sent her heart rate into a thumping beat.

The dark room did nothing to soothe her fears. If anything, the shadows drilled it farther into her bones. Hunter's presence hung in the air, and just as her eyelids finally slid closed, his low, malignant chuckle filled her ears.

Her eyes flew open to the darkness, and the monitor registered her high-speed heartbeat.

"They won't help you this time." His voice caressed her skin like a dozen finely sharpened knives.

"You can't touch me," she whispered. She prayed both the talisman around her neck and the salt line around the bed that Tom had made before he rolled Austin out of the room would prevent Hunter from hurting her.

The temperature in the room dropped into the frigid zone, and she shivered.

"I brought a friend this time," he said.

Her heart squeezed as the chair slid across the room and jammed under the doorknob, locking her in with the crazed ghost and locking out any chance for help.

"Why won't you just go rot in hell?" Paige said through chattering teeth.

"Because I'm here to drag you there with me." His form materialized in the room, solid enough to see his green eyes glaring in her direction before he shimmered and faded.

The air inside the room swirled like a building tornado, and the light from the hallway faded for a moment. The door handle jiggled but wouldn't open with the way the chair was wedged. The nurse's eyes appeared in the small window, and they widened before she stepped away.

Paige tried to scream over the howling wind, but her voice was drowned by the screeching of equipment sliding across the floor. She glanced down at the salt line, and her heart thundered louder than the wind. Salt grains moved, thinning the line, and once it was breached, she knew Hunter and whomever he brought with him would do unspeakable things.

With each grain that trailed away, her level of fear increased until she found it difficult to draw a breath. The pounding on the door pulled her attention from the dwindling line of protection, and her gaze met Austin's through the glass.

"Help me!"

Even though she knew he couldn't hear over the storm in her room, he nodded and brought a phone to his ear.

Paige's gaze blurred, and she blinked the hot tears from her eyes. The last kernel of salt blew to the side, leaving a breach in her protection. The wind in the room silenced. Only her ragged breathing remained as she stared at Austin's panicked gaze.

A hand wrapped around her throat, pulling her forwards. In the darkness, Hunter's green eyes shimmered.

"I thought about letting them fuck you to death while lover boy watched, but I think it would tear him up more to see you bleed," Hunter's voice whispered in her ear. "And while I promised Max and the boys a good fucking, if they came along, they will have to wait until I'm done with you."

Paige didn't have a chance to speak before Hunter hurled her across the room. The IV in her forearm tore out, leaving a painful gash, and the impact with the wall dazed her. Blood flowed from the cut and the pain from her previous beatings flared, drawing her breath in and locking the air in her chest.

Her gaze darted around the dark as she got to her hands and knees. Austin's yell from the other side of the door sounded distant among the buzzing in her ears. Icy hands gripped her arms and lifted her off her feet, slamming her against the wall with such force, she let out a yelp.

"I want you in agony." His voice pierced her, and then she was flying through the air again.

She hit the side of the bed and sent it crashing into the wall. The snap in her arm was as audible as the scream that came out of her lips. Cradling her broken and bleeding appendage, she tried to crawl into the corner, but icy hands dragged her back to the center of the floor before grasping her hair and pulling her to her knees, facing the door.

Paige's arm throbbed and tears blurred her vision, but she saw enough horror in Austin's eyes to shatter her soul. The pain hadn't reached the blackout level, but she knew Hunter wouldn't let her get to that land of bliss.

The punch to her kidney pulled a scream from her, and she arched away from the pain. The grip on her hair released, and then the sting of a backhand sent her onto the ground again. She caught herself with her broken arm and cried out at the sharp pain radiating all the way to her shoulder. She fell face first into the tile.

Sobbing, she attempted to get to her hands and knees when a foot connected with her side, spinning her onto her back. White spots filled her vision, and a hand clasped her neck, lifting her off the ground before tossing her on the bed. She landed on her stomach across it, but even the soft mattress couldn't absorb the pain of the impact.

"Have at her, boys," Hunter growled.

Hands rolled her onto her back and clawed at the hospital gown wrapped around her. Her attempts to wiggle away were futile. The ripping of fabric was shadowed by the slam of the door against the wall. All movement stopped as two figures stood side by side, backlit by the hall light.

Paige blinked at them and Austin beyond them, along with the panicked night nurse.

"Let her go," the voice in the doorway commanded.

Hunter laughed and his form materialized in the room. "You can't stop us."

Paige got a good look at the two men when they stepped closer. The door slammed behind them, but neither Tom nor the man next to him reacted.

"Hold that thought," the man next to Tom said as he turned his gaze from Hunter to Paige.

White flared around her and she closed her eyes against the brightness while screams filled her ears. She curled onto her side and tried to cover both ears, but her broken arm would not cooperate. When the light faded along with the screams, she blinked her eyes open.

Both Tom and the stranger were engaged in a staring contest with Hunter as he rattled off some ancient hex.

It wasn't until the man next to Tom smirked that recognition set in. CJ Ryan, the famous singer, was standing in her hospital room. He glanced in her direction as the thought barreled through her mind before he returned all his attention to the now solid form of Hunter Garrett.

Every sharp object in the room rose from the floor and aimed in Paige's direction. Hunter smiled in satisfaction as he snapped his fingers and they launched at her. Austin screamed in the background, but neither Tom nor CJ moved.

Paige covered her head, and the flair of white light engulfed the room. The heat from it brushed her skin, and Hunter's angry bellow followed. She squinted into the light and swallowed hard at the sight of the white fire engulfing the ghost. Hunter fought it, but it overwhelmed him until nothing was left but dust. As the light faded, the dust blew in a small swirl before it disappeared altogether.

The door burst open, and Austin was across the room in seconds. Paige met his gaze as tears tumbled from her eyes, leaving hot streaks that pooled in her ears.

The nurse marched into the room and tried to move Austin away, but the glare he leveled in her direction made her hesitate.

"We'll be taking her out of here," CJ said as both he and Tom approached the bed. "For her safety," he added when the nurse sent her sharp stare in his direction.

Paige focused on him and the way he stared down at the nurse.

"You saw the assailant get away and had both Miss Turner and Mr. Shelton moved for their safety," he whispered.

When the nurse blinked, nodded, and shuffled out of the room, CJ turned towards Paige. "Tom, you'll need to carry her. I don't think your friend is in any condition to do that." He turned and walked out of the room.

Tom scooped her into his arms as gently as possible, and she leaned into his solid but soft frame, feeling safe for the first time since they had left home.

Austin smoothed her hair out of her face and glanced up at Tom. "Where are we going?"

"Back to the apartment," CJ said from the doorway. "My wife is a doctor."

Paige closed her eyes, grinding her teeth against the pain. Every step jostled her into the world of agony, and she pressed her lips against the sobs that begged to escape.

When Tom set her down in the car, the pain overwhelmed her, and she let a whine escape. He offered her a sad smile and his eyes reflected the apology without words. Austin slid into the seat next to her. The slam of the trunk shook the car, and then CJ slid behind the wheel.

"You're going to be okay," Austin said as he pulled her against him.

"I'm not so sure," Paige whispered.

"They promised me you'd be okay," he whispered in her ear. "And after what I just witnessed, I think they can make good on that promise."

She glanced at him, but he was staring at the driver with such reverence that she smiled, despite the pain that caused in her cheeks.

# Black Magick
## Chapter 15

"JESUS, CHRIS, WHAT the hell were you thinking?" Her voice pierced the cracked door. "We don't even know these people."

"Look, Sarah's brother brought him here, figuring we might be able to help." Steve Williams argued with CJ Ryan's wife in the hallway outside the room.

"I told you it was only a matter of time before this demon spirit came back for them. He was stronger than anything I've felt since..." Raven's Irish brogue trailed off. "Angel fire was our only option to save that girl."

"How many people saw what Chris did?" CJ's wife spat back.

Austin traded a glance with Paige. Her eyes reflected that dull look of extreme pain, and he just wanted it to go away. The discomfort he felt was nothing in comparison, and he forced himself to his feet and crossed to the door, opening it.

"Just the night nurse, Mrs. Ryan," Austin answered, echoing what CJ had just said. "Paige needs help," he added, staring at CJ's wife. "Can you help her or not?"

She studied him and sighed, her eyes softening. "Yes. I can help her," she said with a nod. "You aren't doing too well yourself," she added.

"I'll live," he said and stepped aside, waving her into the room.

Valerie Ryan tucked her hair behind her ears and stepped into the room. She crossed and took a seat on the edge of the bed.

"Who are you people?" Paige whispered.

Valerie smiled at her and glanced over at Austin with a sigh. "This might hurt a bit," she said and leaned forward, placing a simple kiss on Paige's forehead.

Austin stared as Paige gasped, her body arching in the type of pain one only sees in the dying while trying to cling to life. Her eyes rolled back, and she slumped back onto the bed. Austin moved towards her side, but before he reached the bed, sparks surrounded Paige. He stopped a few steps from the bed and stared as the light encompassed her. It seeped into her skin, illuminating her entire form. The bruises stood out against the translucent light until they faded.

Her broken arm moved, bone scraping and resetting. The bloody welt from the torn IV line mended until nothing was left. As the light faded, he stared dumbfounded at Paige. Not a mark was left on her skin.

His gaze bounced to CJ's wife. "Who are you?" he whispered, echoing Paige's last question.

She smiled and stood, crossing to him. "We are made from the blood of angels," she whispered and planted a kiss on his cheek.

Blinding pain ripped through his chest and back, and he stumbled, catching himself on the side of the bed. He sank to his knees, clinging to consciousness by the barest of threads as the welts in his back thatched together. The pain of being whipped was minor compared to the magic flowing through his body, and he panted against the need to drop into the black.

After a few moments, his breathing slowed, and the sharp pain subsided to a dull tingle. He glanced at the crowd gathered in the doorway and then up at Valerie Ryan as he pushed himself to his feet.

"After what I saw, I guess that's as believable as anything else," he said.

"I give you props. Usually that renders folks unconscious," Steve said from the doorway.

Austin chuckled and shrugged, swiping the sweat from his forehead and wiping it on the cloth of his hospital gown. He blinked at his attire.

"You wouldn't happen..."

"To have clothes that might fit?" Steve finished.

"Yeah, I'm afraid there isn't much to salvage from my suitcase." He waved toward the small suitcase in the corner of the room.

"Hang on."

Steve came back a few seconds later with sweats, socks, and a Brooksfield University t-shirt, along with an unopened bag of boxers.

"My wife picked those up last week, and I hadn't gotten around to opening them yet," he said, handing the clothing over and taking leave so Austin could get dressed in peace.

Austin didn't second guess the sizes. He took his new bounty into the adjoining bathroom and untied the hospital gown. When it dropped to the floor, he stared at the bandage on his upper left chest. He peeled the gauze away from his skin and blinked. Not even the slightest of scars was visible. His fingers grazed the spot, and a phantom twinge hit, like the injury was there, somewhere, aching to remind him of the horrors he'd endured.

He turned and stared at the pattern of bandages splayed across his back. With what felt like a contortionist's movements, he peeled each one away to display flawless skin. He dropped everything in the garbage before stepping into the shower to wash away all remnants of his scars. Then he wandered into the quiet living room and stared out over the city.

"Kind of tough to absorb, isn't it?"

He turned and met Steve Williams's gaze.

"Where is everyone?"

"They headed back to the concert now that the danger is gone." He offered a shrug. "Care for a drink?" he asked, waving toward the corner bar.

Austin let out a little laugh and nodded. "The stronger, the better."

Steve poured two scotches and handed one to Austin. He knocked it back like a shot and closed his eyes as the warmth spread through his center. He handed the glass back.

"Brooksfield U?" he asked, pointing to his shirt.

"Yeah, that's where I met my wife." He took a seat. "I'm sure you have more pertinent questions than that," he added.

Austin looked away from the incredible view. "I don't even know where to begin."

Steve huffed a laugh and leaned back.

"Ghosts, psychics, witchcraft, and now blood of angels? All I can say is, what the fuck?"

Steve's laugh caught on and turned into a belted guffaw. Austin felt his lips twitch into a smile in response.

"She will buy it more readily than I." Austin pointed toward the hallway before taking a seat on the plush couch. His hand absently swiped the spot where the knife had cut into his skin. "And I don't know how..." he started and trailed off before meeting Steve's gaze.

Steve leaned forward, resting his elbows on his knees as he placed his glass on the table. "I want to stress how important it is not to let any of this get into the public's hands."

Austin tilted his head. "You think..."

Steve's hand came up in the universal symbol for stop. "I don't know, but I've been protecting those two boys since they were kids, and I'm not stopping now." His gaze hardened a little.

"Look, I've witnessed a ghost kill a fraternity full of guys. That same ghost decided I was his best bet for getting his girlfriend back and tricked me into letting him possess my sorry ass. And that seems almost believable compared to this. Who the hell am I going to tell about this shit without ending up in a padded cell?"

Steve leaned back in his seat, his features relaxing before he raised his glass and took a healthy sip of scotch.

Austin's gaze moved back to the city skyline. "Why us?" He shifted in his seat when his gaze returned to Steve. He noted the tilt of his head.

"Tom said you had a good heart," he finally said.

It was Austin's turn to huff. "I don't think so."

"Where are we?" Paige's soft voice pulled his attention to the hallway where she stood. She had the shredded hospital gown wrapped around herself.

Austin stood and crossed to her. "We're still in Manhattan," he said, and her eyes widened, filling with fear faster than he could blink.

"It's okay, he's gone."

Paige's blue eyes caught his, and her blinking increased as Austin's words settled. "I must have been dreaming..."

He slowly shook his head. "It was all real," he said and tucked a stray hair behind her ear.

"Raven left some clothes that might fit her," Steve said.

Paige stiffened, her gaze shooting from Austin to where Steve sat in the shadows.

"Come on. Let's get you dressed, and then I'll fill you in," he said and led Paige back to the bedroom. "You might want a shower before you dress," he said, his gaze finding the traces of blood still smeared on her skin.

Paige followed his gaze and stared at the bloodstained skin of her arm before her head snapped up to stare at him. She turned and stepped into the brightly lit bathroom and stepped in front of the mirror, ripping the cloth off her body. She stared, much as he had, at her perfectly unblemished skin.

Austin leaned against the doorjamb, waiting for her to meet his gaze. She even turned around to find the whip welts, but there was nothing but soft skin. She turned towards him with wide eyes and spread her arms, asking the question without words.

He offered her a ghost of a smile and a shrug. "I seem to have made the right kind of friends," he said.

She let out a hysterical, high-pitched laugh before her chin trembled.

Austin stepped into the room and pulled her into his arms.

"It's like it never happened," she sobbed. "But I know it did. I know I was beaten and raped by the monster."

He smoothed her hair and whispered, "Shhh" into her ear while she shook in his arms. He kept his eyes open, because if he closed them, all he would see was her flying across the hospital room screaming for him while he remained locked out and helpless. His eyes stung, and he blinked, tightening his grip on her so he wouldn't start shaking right along with her.

She pulled away, looking up at him. Her teary eyes widened, and her soft hand cupped his cheek, her thumb wiping his tears away.

"I couldn't do a damned thing," he said, his voice shaking in a way he hated. But he was as helpless to stop the aftershock as he was of stopping Hunter's ghost.

"But you did. You called in the cavalry."

He huffed and shrugged at the same time.

"I'd just like to know if what I think I saw was real."

"You saw an angel, didn't you?" he asked, because what he saw happen in that room couldn't have been real unless she saw the same thing.

She laughed and blushed a little. "I thought I saw that famous singer that I love, but yeah, he looked like an angel, with wings and all."

"Take a shower. I'll bring the clothes in here, and then we can talk with Mr. Williams." He stepped out of the bathroom, crossed to the pile of clothing on the bureau, and brought it back into the bathroom while Paige rinsed in the shower.

She stepped out a few minutes later and dried off before slipping on the clothing he handed her. As each article was pulled on, another perfectly smooth, unblemished part of her body was covered.

While she didn't sport any injuries on the surface, inside, she was as damaged as he was.

She wrung out her hair and then hand-combed it before meeting his gaze. In her vibrant blue irises, he saw the soul-crushing pain, and he offered what he hoped was a smile, took her hand, and lead her into the living room where Steve still sat. There were now three glasses on the coffee table, each filled halfway with golden scotch.

"I figured you would need a drink." He nodded toward the glasses.

Austin took both glasses and handed one to Paige as they sat on the couch together.

After they each took a sip, Steve leaned forward, extending his hand. "I'm Steve," he said.

Paige shook his hand. "Steve... Williams?" she asked, tilting her head like she did when she was thinking.

He nodded.

"Special Agent Williams?" she asked as her eyes rounded wide.

"Former. Yes." He leaned back in the seat.

Austin glanced at Paige, and she met his gaze. Pure awe cascaded down her face until her mouth popped open. And he knew he was missing something significant.

"You don't remember the news stories?" she whispered.

Austin shrugged, but before he could try to answer, the front door opened, and the rest of the family poured into the apartment.

Paige's eyes widened farther at the first one into the room.

"Oh, my god. I wasn't dreaming," Paige said, and her head whipped back towards Austin. "That's CJ Ryan!" She pointed and her hand shook as much of the rest of her, but it wasn't based on fear. Instead, it was more of the fan girl he knew she was at heart.

Austin grinned and stood.

"I never got a chance to thank you," he said and stuck out his hand.

"Anytime. It's what we do," CJ said, and clasped Austin's hand in a solid handshake.

Austin glanced behind him. "And thank you as well. I don't know what kind of magic you spun, but it saved her life, so you will always have my gratitude."

"As my husband said, it's what we do, so my pleasure," Valerie said in a soft voice, and held a key out to Austin. "We got you a room at the Plaza."

"I...uh...," Austin said, staring at the key.

"And some new clothes," Raven said from behind the group, stepping into the line of sight with Tom.

Tom pulled out a card and handed it to Austin before signing.

"He said we should call them if we run into trouble or if either of us needs to talk. They've all been where we are, so..." Austin translated and then looked at the card. The logo for a paranormal research firm stood out in stark contrast to the handwritten phone number beside the office number.

"Thank you," Paige said, finding her voice.

CJ paused at the entrance to the hallway and turned. "Your parents really named you Paige?" he asked with a smirk.

Paige blushed and nodded.

"Do you have a middle name?"

"No. It's just Paige. Paige Turner," she said, and a smirk found her lips. It found everyone's lips.

CJ Ryan smiled, scribbled something, and then tossed a compact disc to Paige.

Austin glanced at the note. *To the girl whose name will always make me smile. It was a pleasure meeting you, Paige. Next time I'm playing in the city, I'll make sure you and Austin have front row seats. CJ Ryan.*

She glanced up from the signed CD like it was a shiny diamond instead of just a collection of his best music, and then looked at Austin. For whatever it was worth, the words pulled the shine back into her eyes, and Austin smiled, thanking whoever was up above for sparing her.

"Well, I'll just grab our things," Austin said and headed to the room to collect what little they had left.

CJ caught him at the door, his expression dead serious as his eyes penetrated the deepest part of his soul.

"It's going to be a long, hellish road back," he started, but Austin stopped him by raising his hand.

"I know, and it might tear us apart in the end."

CJ's lips twitched into a smile. "Only if you let it. And if you do, he wins."

The shock of his words was like a jolt of electricity, and he jerked a step back. "Why do you even care?"

CJ glanced over his shoulder for a moment before returning his gaze. "I recognize angel blood when I see it. It's one of the few things I'll risk my ass for these days," he said and walked away.

Austin stood frozen to the spot, and then his gaze traveled toward the living room. "Who?" he asked, thinking about the color of Paige's eyes. It seemed to be in the same color palate as both Tom and CJ.

CJ stopped before he stepped into the bedroom at the end of the hall and turned in his direction. "Paige isn't a descendant," he said, reading Austin's mind accurately. "She's just a very talented Wiccan, like my brother's wife."

The suitcase fell out of Austin's grip as he stared at CJ Ryan, the man who wielded angel wings and annihilated the evil hurting Paige. His index finger slowly pointed at his own chest. When CJ smiled and gave a shrug before disappearing, he nearly sat on his ass in shock.

"What the hell does that even mean?" he asked no one in particular.

# Black Magick
# Chapter 16

AUSTIN STARED OUT the window of The Plaza Hotel, focusing on nothing as Paige shuffled through the television channels. The news story she stopped on pulled his attention to the television. It was the report of what happened to them, including the so-called attack at the hospital.

When Detective Connolly stepped into the shot to make a statement, Austin took a seat and listened as the facts poured out. The only thing not included was that Paige had killed Hunter. Instead, they catalogued it as a suicide.

Paige turned toward Austin, her eyes wide and her mouth open in the same kind of shock radiating through him.

"Did they?" she asked, pointing toward the window.

"I honestly don't know, Paige. Detective Connolly was so shaken by what happened to him at the hospital that he just might have done that one on his own." He glanced at the television and back at Paige. "Either way, it makes both of us free and clear of any wrongdoing." He added a shrug for emphasis. "So, we're free to go home after we get a decent night's sleep."

"I'm not sure I'll ever sleep again," Paige mumbled.

He slid into bed next to her and pulled her into the nook of his arm. "We will, eventually," he said and kissed her forehead. "Until then, I'll do my best to keep the nightmares away."

She looked up from his chest, and a tear spilled down her cheek. She didn't need to say the words because they reflected as clearly as the sunrise over the city, but when the shaking words whispered between them, he smiled at the ones left unspoken.

"Thank you for not giving up."

"Baby, I could never give up on you," he said and gently planted a kiss on her cheek. "How would you feel if I applied to Dartmouth?"

She blinked at him and shifted onto her elbow. "But your dreams..."

He shut her up with a kiss and then said, "Dartmouth has a decent medical program. Besides, you're there, and if I'm being honest here, you are my real dream."

"Even after all this?"

"Especially after all this," he said and tucked a strand of hair behind her ear.

Paige seemed to curl into herself, and her gaze dropped between them. "You know what they did to me."

"Yes. But you aren't the only one damaged by this," he said softly, and her gaze lifted. "I couldn't stop what happened any more than you could, and that's going to eat away at me. Just the way what they did will tear you apart inside."

"So, why go through that pain?" she asked, and a little part of him died inside.

"We have something here, right?" He wasn't sure he wanted to hear the answer, but her tentative nod sparked his hope. "Do you trust me?"

She blinked at the question, and her chin trembled. "I trust you with my life," she said, and her husky voice cracked, making it sexier than normal. "But I'm not sure I can give you everything you want."

"What is it you think I want?" he asked, using his softest, calmest voice despite the aggravation eating away at his stomach.

She dropped her gaze to his chest, avoiding his eyes. "Sex," she whispered.

His head fell onto the pillow, and he stared at the ceiling, silently counting down from ten in order to make his voice calm and devoid of anger.

"Is that really all you think I want from you?" he asked without looking at her. She didn't answer, and he stifled the urge to growl out a swear word or two. When he finally made himself look at her, the tears were spilling down her cheeks, and she was looking out the window instead of at him. "The past few months I didn't make a move because I needed to know this was more than just the bedroom connection, because

God knows we have the sex thing down to a science."

Her head snapped towards him.

"You wanted to know why I didn't touch you? It's because I didn't trust what I was feeling. I had to be sure it wasn't just a sex thing."

She stared at him.

"And I basically asked you to move in with me at the hotel, so that should give you a clue about what's really important to me."

"You still..." She couldn't finish her statement and she sat up, wrapping her arms around her legs.

"If we let this fall to pieces, then that fucker wins, and there is no way I'm going to let that happen. You know why?"

Tears spilled, and she shook her head, still looking out at the city lights.

"Because I fucking love you. That's why."

Her chin trembled, and she buried her face in her hands. Each sob ripped through him, and he sat up, wrapping his arms around her and pulling her into his lap. Her arms snaked around him, and she cried into his shoulder, clinging to him like if she let go, he might disappear like a wisp of smoke.

After what seemed like forever, she picked up her head and met his gaze.

"I'm such a mess," she said, wiping her face.

"Yeah, you are, but I'm not exactly the rock of stability, either."

She uttered a soft laugh and pressed her lips to his. "You're more of a rock than you know." Her breath tickled against his lips, and when she pulled away, she met his gaze.

"I think this, what we have, is worth it," he said.

Her eyebrow cocked. "You think?" she asked with a teasing sniffle.

"Yeah. I think. As long as we're both in the same place."

Her hand caressed his cheek as she stared into his eyes, and he bit his tongue, avoiding asking her the direct question. He wanted her to say it of her own accord, and he was afraid he may have already pushed it too far. When she leaned her forehead against his, he swallowed the disappointment.

"I didn't realize how far gone I was until..." she said and paused, taking a deep breath before continuing, "… until I thought I'd lost you."

He pulled away, and their eyes met. She leaned in, delivering a soft kiss with a spark behind it. He let it morph into more, and their tongues mingled, intimate and tender, tangling in a slow roll that took his breath away. It was the type of kiss that promised more, but he also knew now wasn't the time to explore the boundaries.

He broke the kiss and pulled a slow breath before opening his eyes to hers.

"I am in the same place, Austin, but I'm afraid that might not be enough."

He smiled, cocking his head while he kept her gaze. "I can't promise you it will be easy, but I can promise it will be worth the fight."

The End

Continue Paige and Austin's story with Practical Magick.

# ABOUT J.E. TAYLOR

J.E. Taylor is a USA Today bestselling author, a publisher, an editor, a manuscript formatter, a mother, a wife, a business analyst, and a Supernatural fangirl. Not necessarily in that order. She first sat down to seriously write in February of 2007 after her daughter asked:

"Mom, if you could do anything, what would you do?"
From that moment on, she hasn't looked back.

Besides being co-owner of Novel Concept Publishing, Ms. Taylor also moonlights as a Senior Editor of Allegory E-zine, an online venue for Science Fiction, Fantasy and Horror, and co-host of the popular YouTube talk show Spilling Ink.

She lives in New Hampshire with her husband and during the summer months enjoys her weekends on the shore in southern Maine.

Visit her at www.jetaylor75.com to check out her other titles and sign up for her newsletter for early previews of her upcoming books, release announcements, and special opportunities for free swag!

# MAGICK TRILOGY

Accused of overdosing her fiancé, Paige Turner must clear her name. But with all the evidence pointing in her direction, proving her innocence may be an impossible feat, especially since she's locked up in a sanitarium.

To make matters worse, her dead fiancé doesn't want to move on. He is happy to haunt her until Austin, an orderly at the hospital, takes notice of

Paige, and she responds to his attention.

Then her fiancé's ghost becomes enraged. And there is nothing simple about dealing with an angry spirit in an insane asylum.

When the ghost takes possession of Austin, Paige must figure out a way to free him before her fiancé takes over for good. But banishing a ghost is tricky, especially when her magick skills are rusty.

Will her spell save Austin?

Or will it just transplant the furious ghost into a different body, one primed for revenge, and doom them both?

This trilogy includes the following books:

**Magick**

**Black Magick**

**Practical Magick**

Find these titles and other fantasy
and suspense titles on J.E. Taylor's
website!

www.JETaylor75.com